A Christmas Prayer

Also by Kimberla Lawson Roby

THE REVEREND CURTIS BLACK SERIES

The Prodigal Son
A House Divided
The Reverend's Wife
Love, Honor, and Betray
Be Careful What You Pray For
The Best of Everything
Sin No More
Love & Lies
The Best-Kept Secret
Too Much of a Good Thing
Casting the First Stone

STANDALONE TITLES

The Perfect Marriage
Secret Obsession
A Deep Dark Secret
One in a Million
Changing Faces
A Taste of Reality
It's a Thin Line
Here & Now
Behind Closed Doors

A Christmas Prayer

KIMBERLA LAWSON ROBY

GRAND CENTRAL
PUBLISHING

NEW YORK   BOSTON

Grand Central Publishing
Hachette Book Group
1290 Avenue of the Americas
New York, NY 10104

www.HachetteBookGroup.com

Printed in the United States of America

RRD-C

First Edition: October 2014

10 9 8 7 6 5 4 3 2 1

Grand Central Publishing is a division of Hachette Book Group, Inc. The Grand Central Publishing name and logo is a trademark of Hachette Book Group, Inc.

The Hachette Speakers Bureau provides a wide range of authors for speaking events. To find out more, go to www.hachettespeakersbureau.com or call (866) 376-6591.

The publisher is not responsible for websites (or their content) that are not owned by the publisher.

Library of Congress Cataloging-in-Publication Data has been applied for.

Will M. Roby, Jr.
Thank you for being my soul mate,
my confidant, my best friend.
Thank you for loving me so unconditionally.
Thank you for being the
best husband in the world.
I love you with all my heart.

Arletha Tennin Stapleton
Thank you for all your genuine love,
for all the happy times at Christmas
and for all the huge family dinners.
Thank you for being the absolute best mom ever.
I miss you so very much, and
I will love you always.

A Christmas Prayer

Chapter 1

It was Black Friday, and while millions of folks were out chasing some of the most colossal deals of the century, all Alexis wanted was for this whole Christmas season to be over with. There were times when she wished she could feel differently, but ever since her mom had passed away five years ago, she hadn't wanted anything to do with it. Of course, she did still recognize and mentally rejoice at the beautiful birth of Christ, but when it came to huge family celebrations and festive gatherings, she wanted no parts of them. What she did instead, mostly, was pray that New Year's Day would come as quickly as possible so she could get on with her life.

Alexis curled her body into a tighter ball, picked up the remote control, and looked toward the flat-screen television on her bedroom wall. It was shortly past one in the afternoon, yet she still lay in her dark mahogany sleigh-style bed with her pajamas on. She just didn't feel like doing anything, and the fact that almost about every news channel she turned to showed massive shopping crowds and footage of customers and workers being trampled, well, that made Alexis want to turn off the TV altogether. As it was, she had already been trying her best to avoid every one of those sappy Hallmark Christmas card commercials, and she'd certainly been staying clear of one of her personal favorites—the Hallmark Channel itself, since they were doing what they did every year: airing those depressing Christmas movies day in and day out, twenty-four/seven.

If only her mom were still here, Alexis would be so much happier. Even now, she couldn't help thinking about how much her mom had loved, loved, loved Christmas. It had been by far her favorite holiday, and she'd adored it so much that she would immediately begin decorating the day after Thanksgiving. She would celebrate in various other ways, too, the entire month of December, including playing some of her favorite Christmas carols, such as "Silent Night," "Away in a Manger," and "The First Noel." Then, on the twenty-fifth, she would host a huge family dinner. She bought gifts for everyone, she baked and cooked and baked and cooked some more, and on Christmas afternoon, she would say, "I almost hate to see the sun go down, because Christmas will just about be over."

This was how it had always been, and it was because of these kinds of sentiments that Alexis was full of happy childhood memories. She even had fond memories from her adult life...that is, until her mom had passed. Now her heart was consumed only with sadness.

Alexis flipped through more channels, sighing heavily. But then she came upon one of her favorite movies, *This Christmas*, starring Loretta Devine, Regina King, and Idris Elba. She could tell the movie had been on for a while because Chris Brown was already walking toward the front of the church, preparing to sing . . . "This Christmas." Alexis watched and listened, though she wasn't sure why she tortured herself this way, because not once had she ever watched this scene without breaking into tears. It was such a reminder of her mom and the way she had loved and doted on her family. It also reminded Alexis of how her mom had taught her children exceedingly strong Christian values. She'd raised Alexis and her younger sister, Sabrina, to treat all people the way they wanted to be treated and to keep God and family first in their lives. The two of them had been very blessed to have such a loving, caring, and compassionate mother—and it meant everything.

Alexis watched Chris Brown singing from the depths of his soul and then saw family members standing and walking into the church aisle, embracing one another. It was after this that Alexis's eyes welled up with tears, and she cried uncontrollably. She missed her mother so tremendously that her chest ached. Then, to make matters worse, the next scene showcased the entire family gathered around the dinner table. They looked as though they couldn't be happier, and Alexis couldn't help thinking how this was the way she'd once felt, too.

But as the saying went, that was then and this was

now. Her mother was gone, and as far as Alexis was concerned, there wasn't a single thing or person that could make her feel better about it, not even the people Alexis loved. Paula, her best friend since childhood, had been trying to lift her Christmas spirit for years, and so had Alexis's fiancé, Chase, for the time he'd known her. But if anything, Alexis seemed to feel sadder with each passing year. In fact, this year she'd begun dreading the whole idea of Christmas as early as September. She wasn't sure what had set her off exactly; all she knew was that not long after Labor Day, the thought of Christmas had entered her mind and she'd become depressed. It was as if the simplest anticipation of it all had been enough to ruin Alexis's day, which was the reason she'd taken that particular afternoon off. This hadn't been hard to do, since she was self-employed as a motivational speaker and her hours were flexible, but she still hated that mere thoughts of Christmas affected her so gravely.

It also didn't help that she and her sister, Sabrina, were usually at odds about one thing or another. Alexis and Sabrina had never gotten along the way sisters should. They were just too different, she guessed. But at least when their mom had been alive, they'd worked harder at it and tolerated each other more. Now, Alexis practically had to beg to see her niece, Courtney, and there were times when Sabrina still told her no just to be spiteful. The two of them had a lot of bad history, but that was a whole other story and one Alexis didn't want to think about because it was far too distressing.

As one thought after another raced through her mind, Alexis wept like a child. She was miserable, and she wished she could sleep for the next week. She knew this wasn't logical, but she just wanted this awful pain to go away. She wanted to be at peace, and before long, she glanced over at the bottle of amitriptyline on her wooden nightstand. Her doctor had prescribed it for insomnia, and although she only took one ten-milligram pill at bedtime, and sometimes only half a pill, she contemplated taking much more. Or maybe all she needed to do was take two of them, because she knew one woman who took twenty-five milligrams for unexplained abdominal pain and another who took more than that for depression. If Alexis only took twenty milligrams, she wouldn't be overdoing it, and she also wouldn't likely wake up until many hours from now—meaning she wouldn't have to think about the loss of her mom or anything relating to family or Christmas. She would simply be able to sleep away her sadness, and by tomorrow, Black Friday and all the hoopla surrounding it would be over. She was sure the media would continue covering all the shopping stories throughout the weekend as well as on Cyber Monday, but at least the biggest shopping day of the year would have ended, and she'd be one day closer to January 1.

All she had to do was bide her time, and things would return to normal. They had to, because after all, she and Chase were getting married in June, and the last thing she wanted was to be an unhappy bride. She was engaged to the man of her dreams, and she looked forward to becoming Mrs. Chase Dupont III. This was what she kept telling herself, anyway—especially since her future mother-in-law was the most heartless woman she'd ever met. Still, what woman in her right mind wouldn't be thrilled about marrying a man like Chase? He was gorgeous, well educated, and CEO of a Fortune 500 company called Borg-Freeman Technologies—which, interestingly enough, was the same position his father had held for years before his passing. He'd also placed a five-karat ring on her finger, and he truly loved her. By most people's standards, Chase was everything a woman could hope for, so Alexis tried to remember that.

But for now, she reached over and picked up her pill bottle, opened it, swallowed two pills with water, and lay back down. She closed her eyes and smiled. In a few moments, she'd be sound asleep and wouldn't have to think about Christmas at all...and she certainly wouldn't have to think about Chase's mother—or the disastrous time she'd had with them yesterday during Thanksgiving dinner. She wouldn't have a problem in the world, and just knowing that made her feel better already.

Chapter 2

Alexis stretched her arms toward her headboard, yawned, and opened her eyes. She was still a bit groggy and felt as though she'd been sleeping for days, but she smiled when she saw Chase sitting next to her on the side of her bed.

"Good morning, sleepyhead," he said, smiling.

"Good morning," she said.

"I didn't think you were ever going to wake up. Even when I came by last night, I couldn't get you to say more than a few words."

"You were here?"

"Yeah. I'd been calling you all afternoon, and when you didn't answer I got worried. So when I left work, I decided to drop by. Thank goodness I have a key. You were really out of it, though."

"I was tired."

"Maybe, but I'm sure those sleeping pills had a lot to do with it, too."

Alexis wondered how he knew about those.

"You look surprised. Which means you don't remember anything you told me last night, do you?"

Alexis stared at him but didn't say anything.

"You said you only took two of them, but if you can't even remember our conversation, then that must be some very strong medicine."

"I just wanted to sleep."

Chase caressed the side of her face. "I know this is a tough time for you, and I'm really sorry I had to go in to the office yesterday. I never expected to be there for as long as I was. I didn't get out of there until after six."

"It was fine."

"No, it wasn't. You sounded so sad when I called you yesterday morning, and I should have been here for you."

"It's not a problem, and I'm good now."

"You sure?"

"Positive."

"You wanna go out for breakfast?"

Alexis paused because she didn't feel much like going anywhere, but she still said, "Sounds good to me." Then she flipped the comforter and sheet away from her and sat up. When she stood, Chase pulled her back down beside him.

"What are you doing?" she asked.

"You know," he said, running his hand through her long hair.

"You know the rules, though, right?"

"Yeah, but how about we forget those rules for a change? Just for today."

"Chase—" she began, but then lost her train of thought when he kissed her up and down her neck. "Chase, don't. Breakfast ends at eleven."

"And?"

"You know we can't do this."

"Baby, come on. Just this once."

"No," she said between breaths while pushing him away. "We agreed, remember?"

"Some agreements are made to be broken," he said, unbuttoning her pajama top and kissing her chest.

Alexis closed her eyes and hung her head back, moaning.

"Lexi, please" he begged. "I really wanna make love to you."

She wanted him, too, but she whispered, "No. Baby, it's wrong."

"But remember how good it was when we first met?"

Alexis could barely contain herself, because she actually did remember. She'd never felt better in her life. She hadn't been with a lot of men, but none of them had made her feel as wonderful as Chase had. It also didn't help that he looked so good. She hated to refer to him as tall, dark, and handsome because it was so cliché, but that's exactly what he was. He was six foot two, and he had short coal-black hair with a slight wave to it. Alexis was five foot nine, though, so when she wore heels, that made her love his height even more.

Chase slid her pajama top down her shoulders, lay on top of her, and kissed her on the lips.

But then his phone rang.

Alexis tried to push him away, but he kissed her more intensely.

His phone rang again, and suddenly she heard her home phone ringing, too. When she looked at her caller ID and saw their church's toll-free number, she knew it was a sign from God. Whenever there were new church announcements she received a recorded call, and this one couldn't have come at a better time.

"Baby, I can't do this," she said. "I'm sorry."

Chase looked at her and then lay on his back with his hands over his eyes. "You're killing me."

"I know you don't like this, but I'm just trying to do what's right. And having sex before marriage is wrong."

Chase sighed. "Maybe, but this celibacy thing is driving me crazy, Lexi."

She leaned over and propped her elbow on the bed. "We barely have six months to go, and then you'll never have to go through this again."

"It feels like a decade. But I will say this . . . at least you know for sure that I'm really in love with you."

"Why do you say that?"

"Because I would never deprive myself this way otherwise. I'm suffering like a starved animal."

"Whatever," she said, laughing.

"I'm serious. You have no idea what this feels like. Women can go without for years if they have to, but men? We're in a whole different category."

"Like I said, it won't be long. And anyway, you'd better check to see who called you."

Chase reached across the bed and pulled his phone from his black leather jacket. He must have laid it there while Alexis was asleep.

"It was Mother," he said. "You don't mind if she tags along with us, do you?"

Alexis wanted to scream. It was bad enough that she'd had to spend hours with Mrs. Dupont on Thanksgiving, so the last thing she wanted was to see her again today. Mrs. Dupont—or actually, Geneva, since that's what she insisted Alexis call her—had even gone so far as making disapproving facial expressions when she took a bite of both the yams and the dressing that Alexis had made, even though everyone else had raved about them.

"She's been pretty lonely since my dad passed away, and I sort of feel bad about leaving her alone during the holidays."

Alexis knew a number of women who'd lost their husbands, but none of them had moved in with their children. Chase's dad had passed two years ago, so Alexis wondered why Geneva was still living with Chase. If she'd been ill or didn't have the financial means to take care of herself, Alexis could understand it, but Geneva had a huge mansion of her own and was extremely wealthy. Not to mention, the woman was sixty-five years old and feistier than most forty-year-old women. She was headstrong and noticeably independent, so none of this made sense.

Chase continued. "Since I'm her only child, I'm all she has. But she's definitely moving out before our wedding. She's already promised."

Alexis didn't say anything, but now she was sorry she'd agreed to go to breakfast with him. She fully understood how much Chase loved his mom, and she had the utmost respect for any man who took care of his mother the way Chase did, but Geneva Dupont was a real handful and one of the most controlling mothers Alexis had met. Geneva also didn't seem too fond of the idea that Chase had asked Alexis to marry him, but in front of Chase, she pretended she was ecstatic about it.

Just as Alexis got up to go take a shower, Chase's phone rang again. She knew it was Geneva, because whenever Chase didn't answer his phone, his mother waited maybe five minutes to call him again. Sometimes she called back within seconds. She did this sort of thing all the time, calling him for no reason—especially when she knew he was visiting Alexis or they were out somewhere together.

He finally answered. "Hey, Mother...no, it was in my jacket, and I didn't get to it in time," he said, looking at Alexis.

Alexis shook her head and left the bedroom. She'd do anything to get out of going to breakfast with this woman, but she didn't want to disappoint Chase. All she could hope for was that her time with Geneva wouldn't be as bad as she was imagining. Maybe Geneva would treat her nicely for a change. It would take a miracle, but that's what Alexis was counting on.

Chapter 3

Geneva walked ahead of Chase and Alexis, but then stopped when they approached the entrance of The Tuxson, waiting for Chase to open the door for her. No one would realize it, but what Alexis had figured out months ago was that part of the reason Geneva usually walked so far ahead of them whenever they went out to eat or even to church was because she wanted to make sure Chase opened the door for her *first* and then just held it for Alexis. It was the kind of petty thing that most people wouldn't care the least bit about, but you had to know Geneva to understand it.

As they walked closer to the maître d', Geneva stepped to the side, admiring herself. She glanced down at her red-bottom shoes and then at her black St. John pantsuit, confirming that nothing was out of place. She even stroked both sides of her thick salt-and-pepper mane, which was pulled back in a classic bun. Alexis had never met anyone so vain. The other thing that bothered Alexis was that whenever Geneva went to breakfast, lunch, or dinner with them, it always had to be at The Tuxson. Alexis loved The Tuxson as well, but did they have to go to Mitchell's most exquisite restaurant just to have breakfast? Especially since Mitchell had more than enough mom-and-pop diners to choose from. These were diners that had some of the tastiest food, too. But no. Geneva Dupont wouldn't be caught dead in a place like that, because it was beneath her.

"If you'll follow me," the fiftyish man said.

As they wound their way through a fairly full dining room, Geneva smiled widely and waved at a table full of socialites she'd spied. They smiled and waved back, and there was no mistaking that they were just as uppity as Geneva.

The maître d' pulled out a chair for Geneva, and Chase pulled out the one directly across the table for Alexis.

Geneva sat down and then said, "Why don't you let the man do his job, Chase? He's always trying to help with something." She smiled at the maître d'.

"Uh, yes, ma'am," the man said, clearly feeling awkward. He paused and then said, "Your waitress will be with you shortly."

Wow. So now Geneva didn't want Chase pulling out a chair for Alexis? His own fiancée? This woman was hopeless.

Geneva set her Chanel bag on the empty seat adjacent to her, and just so there wouldn't be any questions or drama about Alexis laying her handbag on top of it,

Alexis hung hers on the back of her chair. She sort of wished they weren't sitting face-to-face, but then Alexis also wouldn't want to sit elbow to elbow with her. So maybe it was best that Chase was slightly sitting between them.

Chase picked up his menu. "They have some great specials today. I think I'll have the rib eye and egg entrée.

"Steak this early in the morning?" Alexis said, scanning her own menu.

"That's the thing about menus," Geneva said without ever looking up to acknowledge Alexis. "They have lots of variety so folks can choose whatever they want."

Alexis took a deep breath. "I wasn't suggesting that Chase not get what he wants. I was just asking a question."

Geneva ignored her and kept looking at her menu.

Chase tried to brighten the mood. "What about you, baby?" he said to Alexis. "What're you having?"

"Not sure yet."

"Hello," a redheaded woman with layers of curly hair said, moving toward and standing between Chase and Geneva. "I'm Pamela, and I'll be your server this morning. Our specials are listed in your menus, but can I start you off with something to drink?"

"I'll have some coffee," Geneva told her.

"I'll have apple juice," Alexis said.

"Coffee for me," Chase added.

"Are you ready to order or do you need a few more minutes?"

Chase looked at Alexis. "Baby, have you decided?"

"Yes, I think so."

"What about you, Mother?" he said.

Geneva nodded and then spoke directly to Pamela. "I believe I'll have your veggie omelet."

"And you?" Pamela said to Alexis.

"I'll have the same."

Geneva locked eyes with Alexis but then quickly looked back at Pamela. "On second thought, I'll take your eggs Benedict."

Alexis wanted to crack up laughing. Geneva was so immature sometimes, and as Alexis looked at Chase she could tell he had no clue that the reason his mother had suddenly changed her mind was because she just couldn't see choosing the same thing Alexis had chosen.

"I'll have the steak and eggs," Chase said.

"With the rib eye or sirloin?"

"Rib eye."

"Sounds good. I'll get this ordered for you right away."

Geneva watched the woman leave the table and pursed her lips. "She's not the classiest person I've seen working here. Good help must be hard to find these days."

"Mother, please," Chase said.

"What? This is a very upscale establishment, and normally they don't hire women like that."

"Like what?"

"Those with tons of wild hair hanging all over the place."

Chase shook his head but then turned to Alexis.

"So how are you feeling?"

"Better—"

"Now, how long has your mother been dead, exactly?" Geneva interrupted. "Did you say five years?"

Alexis swallowed hard. "Yes."

"Didn't you say your dad passed away years ago as well?"

"Yes, he did."

"Hmmm... must be hard having to celebrate the holidays without either of your parents. It's really too bad, because the holidays just don't mean very much when you don't have family."

"Mother," Chase said, leaning back in his chair, "Lexi has plenty of family. She's got her sister and niece and all her aunts and uncles. She also has us."

"It's still not the same as having parents or children. Because if you don't have those, then what's the point?"

Alexis fought back tears, and she was so disappointed in herself for letting this woman get to her this way.

"And anyway," Geneva went on, "why do you keep calling a grown woman Lexi? Her parents named her Alexis, so I would imagine that this is what she prefers to be called."

Chase grabbed Alexis's hand and squeezed it. "It's my pet name for her, Mother, and Lexi doesn't mind me calling her that at all."

Chase smiled at Alexis, but she wanted to sob real tears. All she could think about were her parents, particularly her mother, and how Geneva's words were tearing her apart.

Pamela brought their coffee and juice to the table and walked away again.

Geneva shook her head. "I really should say something to the manager."

"About what?" Chase asked.

"Their hiring practices. They need to stick with clean-cut staff members. It's so much more appropriate."

"Mother, I really wish you wouldn't."

"So, Alexis," Geneva said, ignoring him. "Are you going to the mother-daughter ornament exchange the church is having? Oh, wait a minute." She covered her mouth. "I keep forgetting. You don't have a mother. Can you ever forgive me?"

Alexis pulled her hand away from Chase, snatched her handbag from the chair, and rushed toward the ladies' room. Tears rolled down her face, and once inside she slipped into a stall and closed the door behind her.

If only her mom were here, she wouldn't have to feel this way and not even the likes of Geneva would be able to hurt her. Worse, as much as she loved Chase and wanted to be his wife, she was now having second thoughts about it because of his mother. Alexis just wasn't sure she could continue putting up with all her criticism and rude comments, and she certainly couldn't imagine living under the same roof with that woman. Whenever the subject came up, Chase insisted that Geneva would be moving back to her own home very soon, but Alexis wasn't so sure that would happen.

Alexis sniffled, wiped her face with both hands, and

tried to pull herself together. Then she heard a knock at the door.

"Baby, it's me," Chase said. "Are you okay?"

"I'll be out in a few minutes," she said, glad no one else had come into the bathroom. She knew it was only a matter of time before someone did, so she walked out of the stall.

"I'll wait here for you."

Alexis picked up a napkin from the stack sitting on the vanity, wet it, and patted her face with it. She patted it once more with a dry one and pulled out her pressed face powder sponge to freshen up. Next, she touched up her lipstick, took a deep breath, and left the restroom.

Chase hugged her. "Baby, I'm really sorry about all my mother's questions. I'm sorry for everything she said. Sometimes she just doesn't think."

Alexis hugged him back, but what bothered her was the fact that Chase seemingly had no idea that his mother had made those hurtful comments and asked those questions on purpose. She'd known all along that if she wanted to get the best of Alexis, bringing up the loss of her mother would do it.

They walked back to the table and sat down.

"Alexis, I am so, so sorry that my questions upset you, and I pray you can forgive me. I certainly didn't mean anything by them, and my hope is that once you and Chase are married, you'll see me as your mother figure. Because I would really like that."

Alexis gazed at her and then at Chase, who clearly believed his mother was being genuine. So for the sake of keeping peace, Alexis went along with her future mother-in-law's charade.

"I'd really like that, too," she said, forcing a smile and then looking down at her food. Alexis hadn't meant a word she'd said, though. But neither had Geneva, so as far as Alexis was concerned, they were even—until next time.

Chapter 4

There was nothing like being in the house of the Lord, and Alexis was happy to be at church this morning. She was also glad to have Chase sitting next to her. Incidentally, this was where they'd first met. Their pastor, Reverend Curtis Black, had introduced them during Bible Study, and their chemistry had been immediate. Alexis remembered how she'd barely been able to take her eyes off Chase, and he'd seemed just as smitten with her. To this day, she still wasn't sure why Pastor Black had thought they would be a good match, but a little over a year ago, she'd scheduled a counseling session with him to talk about all the sadness she was still feeling, and he'd ended by saying he wanted her to meet someone. In all honesty, meeting a man had been the last thing she'd wanted to do, what with the number of blind dates she'd gone on that had turned out to be total flops, and it was because of this that she'd basically given up on ever finding her soul mate. But Pastor Black had promised her that if she just gave Chase a chance, she wouldn't be sorry.

Then, as it had turned out, Pastor Black had told Chase that he'd been looking in all the wrong places for the right woman, and that it was time he met the one he was going to marry. Chase had known Pastor Black for years, and although Alexis hadn't been aware of it at the time, Pastor Black was Chase's personal spiritual adviser. Chase was responsible for making countless multimillion-dollar decisions that affected thousands of Borg-Freeman employees, along with the local economy and the company as a whole, and Pastor Black prayed with him and advised him often. It was amazing how much of a difference one year could make, and Alexis would always be thankful to Pastor Black for his wisdom and for bringing them together.

The Deliverance Outreach Mass Choir sang "Grateful," and just like every other time Alexis heard it, tears streamed down her face. It was such a beautiful song, and there were days when she so needed to be reminded of just how blessed she was, she would search YouTube to hear Hezekiah Walker and the Love Fellowship Crusade Choir singing it. She always wept with joy, because it was so easy to focus on problems, when in reality, she just needed to be thankful.

Chase handed her one of his monogrammed handkerchiefs and held her hand. His smile always made her feel better, and she wasn't sure how she could have even considered breaking off their engagement because of his mother. He loved and treated her too well for her to let him go, and somehow she would just have to tolerate Geneva and continue praying that the woman would soon have a change of heart. From the look on her face right now, it wouldn't be today. She was sitting on the other side of Chase, and as soon as she and Alexis made eye contact, she quickly looked away.

When the choir finished, Pastor Black walked up the steps and opened his Bible. He quoted his favorite scripture. "Today is the day the Lord hath made, so let us rejoice and be glad in it."

"Amen," most of the congregation said.

"It is certainly a blessing to stand before you once again on this glorious Sunday morning. I trust that all of you had a wonderful Thanksgiving?"

Members of the church nodded their heads and some answered out loud. Alexis couldn't help thinking about her friend Paula and so many other women in the church who constantly talked about how handsome Pastor Black was. There was no denying that it was true, but Alexis tried her best to focus only on his qualities as her pastor and not on how good he looked.

"Our family did as well," he said, "and although in last week's sermon I did talk quite a bit about being thankful, today I want to talk about what it actually *means* to be grateful. Saying we're grateful and truly *being* grateful are two different things, and sometimes I'm not sure many of us can distinguish one from the other. It's so easy to get caught up in our problems, issues, sad feelings, and the terrible pain we sometimes experience, and this is how we begin to dwell on all the negative aspects of our lives. It becomes the norm for us, and the next thing we know, we find ourselves in a rut. Sometimes the rut is so deep that we can't even hope our way out of it. But the good news is this: Even when we can't hope our way out, we can always pray our way out of anything."

There was thunderous applause and lots of *Amen*s.

"In Matthew seven, verses seven through eight, Jesus says, 'Ask, and it will be given to you; seek, and you will find; knock, and it will be opened to you. For everyone who asks receives, and he who seeks finds, and to him who knocks it will be opened,'" Pastor Black said, turning the pages of his Bible. "And then there's Philippians chapter four, verses six through seven, which says, 'Be anxious for nothing, but in everything by prayer and supplication, with thanksgiving, let your requests be made known to God; and the peace of God, which surpasses all understanding, will guard your hearts and minds through Christ Jesus.' So you see, prayer can and will change everything in your life. There is no problem too large for God, and sometimes I think we tend to forget that, too. There's not a single thing He can't handle, but you have to pray without ceasing. You have to pray and believe and stop holding your own personal pity parties. Life is much too short for that. God wants the best for us, He loves us, and He wants us to be happy."

Alexis nodded and applauded Pastor Black's words along with everyone else. He was so right about all that he was saying, and this was definitely a sermon Alexis needed to hear. She'd just been thinking similar thoughts when the choir was singing, but Pastor Black had brought the whole idea and benefit of prayer to the forefront.

A half hour later, when Pastor Black finished his message and closed his Bible, he said, "Before I end, there's something I want each of you to do. I want you to write a Christmas prayer. I know we've not done anything like this in the past, but this year, I really believe it will help all of us. As you know, the holidays can be hard for those who have lost loved ones. Even for Charlotte and me, last Christmas was the toughest holiday we experienced because we were estranged from our son and grandson. Thank God, they are back with us, but it was then that I realized that loss of any kind can cause major depression and heartache. Then, of course, years ago when we lost our little girl, Marissa, it took what seemed like forever before we fully enjoyed the holidays again. But whether a person is dealing with the loss of a loved one, illness, financial problems, or relationship issues, prayer is always the answer."

*Amen*s echoed throughout the sanctuary.

"I think John fourteen, verse fourteen says it best: 'If ye shall ask anything in my name, I will do it.' So when you write your Christmas prayers, I want you to end them with: Lord, I ask You for this and all other blessings in Your Son Jesus's name, Amen."

Pastor Black spoke a few more words and then gave the

benediction. But just as Chase rested his hand on Alexis's lower back and they stepped into the aisle, Geneva called out to a woman passing by.

"Oh my goodness, Renee, how are you? And needless to say, you're looking as gorgeous as ever. I'm really loving the short haircut."

"You're very kind, Mrs. Dupont. I'm fine, how are you?"

"Doing well, and what's with this Mrs. Dupont thing? Mrs. Dupont was my mother-in-law, and of course, you know I'll always just be Mom when it comes to you."

Geneva was unbelievable. This was obviously Chase's ex, the one he'd dated for a good while but then had broken up with. He'd told Alexis that although Renee had been a nice enough woman, he hadn't been in love with her. But as expected, Geneva still loved everything about her.

"How's it going, Chase?" Renee asked.

"I'm well. You?"

"I'm good."

"And this is Alexis, my fiancée. Alexis, this is Renee."

"Nice to meet you," Renee said.

"Nice to meet you as well."

"We haven't seen you here in ages," Geneva said.

"I know. I've been traveling a lot and visiting other churches."

"Really? Well, I sure hope it's not because of you and Chase. Deliverance Outreach is big enough for all of us. Plus, you will *always* be family to me, no matter what."

Renee smiled. "Thank you for saying that."

"I'm serious. When you and Chase were together, you became the daughter I never had. And nothing or no one," she said, cutting her eyes at Alexis, "will ever change that."

Alexis could barely breathe. She'd stood there for as long as she could, trying to ignore Geneva's messiness, but now she brushed past Chase and went up the aisle and through the first exit she came to.

She heard Chase calling out to her. "Baby, wait."

Alexis kept walking until she made it through the vestibule and outside the building. But Chase caught up to her and grabbed her arm.

Alexis didn't want to make a scene by jerking away from him, so she politely said, "Please let me go."

Chase released her. "Baby, I'm sorry."

Alexis didn't have anything to say, and all she could think about was how her Christmas prayer would now be about something bad happening to her future mother-in-law. But as soon as she fixed her mind on such vicious thoughts, she regretted it and asked God to forgive her. She would never wish any kind of harm on anyone, especially the mother of the man she loved and was going to marry, but it was just that Geneva riled her up in a way like no one had before. And it seemed as though she was getting worse. Maybe she was acting this way because the wedding was only a few months from now, and she was hoping her bullying tactics would force Alexis to break up with Chase. Alexis wasn't sure one way or the other, but she also didn't know how much more of this she could stomach. During service, she'd decided that she wouldn't let anything come between her and Chase, not even his mother, but now she found herself at a crossroads again. So much so that the more she thought about it, the more breaking up with Chase seemed like the only answer. Maybe Geneva would get what she wanted after all, and that would be the end of it.

Chapter 5

It was a new day, and Alexis felt completely refreshed. Last night, she'd taken only one sleeping pill, but it had worked like a charm. She also didn't feel as sad this morning, and she was happy about that. As she lay in bed for a few more seconds, though, she thought about Geneva and the way she'd treated her on Thanksgiving, on Saturday at The Tuxson, and then again yesterday at church. It was the reason Alexis had told Chase she didn't feel well and that she wanted him to drop her off at home, rather than going to dinner with him and his mother. Chase had been noticeably disappointed, but Alexis had been disappointed as well, because he'd still chosen to take his mother out to a restaurant and hadn't gotten back to her house until the evening. Then, of course, with his having to arrive at work pretty early this morning, he hadn't stayed past nine o'clock.

Alexis turned on the television, and just as expected, *CBS This Morning* had on shopping experts who were giving their opinions and predictions about Cyber Monday. They were even comparing the projected sales numbers for this year's Cyber Monday to last year's. Alexis flipped the channel to *Good Morning America*, then to the *Today* show and then to CNN, but every network was covering the same story. The only variation was that there were different hosts and guests on each of them.

Alexis's home phone rang, and she saw that it was Chase. For the first time since meeting him, she debated whether to talk to him.

She sat up and piled three pillows behind her. "Hello?"

"Hi, baby, good morning."

"Morning," she said in a dry tone.

"I know you're still upset, and I can't apologize enough about my mother. Most of the time, she doesn't even realize she's doing anything wrong."

At first Alexis was going to listen and keep quiet, but she couldn't. "Chase, make no mistake about it, your mother is always aware of what she says and does. I don't mean any disrespect to her, but she goes out of her way trying to hurt my feelings all the time. And she does it on purpose."

"Why do you think that?"

"Because it's been happening ever since we first started dating, but after you proposed to me, it got worse. Now it's worse than ever."

"She's just a lonely woman who wants attention."

Alexis didn't bother arguing with Chase any further, because number one, Geneva was his mother, and number two...Geneva was his mother. It just wasn't worth complaining about a man's mother unless he himself saw her for who she was.

"Okay, look," he said, once he realized Alexis had nothing to say. "I'll have a talk with her. Maybe she's just a little jealous. Or maybe she's worried that once we're married, she won't see us much anymore."

Oh, how I wish that were true! Alexis wouldn't dare say that out loud, but she couldn't help thinking it.

"Baby, are you listening?" he asked. "Please don't be upset."

"Yeah, I hear you."

"I'll speak to her as soon as I leave work. Because no matter what my mother says or does, I love you, Lexi, and nothing will ever change that. I need you to believe that, okay?"

"I do believe you, but I also can't take the way your mother treats me. It's too much."

"I promise you, this is going to stop. I didn't realize she was affecting you as much as she has been, and I'm sorry about that. But what I do know is that you are my world, baby, and I'm not sure what I would do without you. Before Pastor Black introduced us, all I cared about was work and more work. It was all I really had, but now you've turned my whole world around for the better. I love you so much it hurts."

Alexis held the phone, speechless and teary-eyed. She heard nothing except sincerity in Chase's voice. How could any woman stay angry with a man like that? Chase truly loved her, and her heart softened completely.

"I love you, too, baby," she said. "More than you could ever possibly know."

"So, now that we have that settled, have you decided on which honeymoon spot we're going to? You know what I prefer, but it's your choice, and we need to get our reservations booked.

"I'm still debating. I know you'd rather go to Italy, but I'm still leaning toward the Caribbean. All I want is to eat well, relax on the beach, and make love to my husband."

"Well, since you put it that way, I say forget Italy!" He laughed. "Let's just go to Half Moon in Jamaica."

"I knew that last part would get your attention. I still can't believe you've never gone anywhere in the Caribbean, though. Especially with all the traveling you've done."

Chase had told her that the reason he'd never gone was because his mother preferred to vacation in places like Milan, Rome, Paris, and London. Even when he was a child, those were the places she and Chase's dad had taken him, and he'd continued vacationing in those same spots as an adult.

Alexis and Chase chatted a few more minutes, but then he had to go.

"I'd better get off of here and head into my meeting. I have a pretty full day."

"I was going to see if you wanted to have lunch, but maybe tomorrow."

"Tomorrow for sure. I'll call you later, though. Love you, baby."

"Love you, too."

Alexis hung up the phone and exhaled. What a whirlwind of emotions she'd been having. She'd gone from being sad to being angry to feeling pretty happy about things again, and it felt good.

She flipped through a few more channels until she landed on a rerun of *Law & Order: SVU*. She hoped this wasn't one of their marathon days, because if it was, she would never get any work done. But just as Stabler and Benson arrested some quack doctor who looked guilty as sin, her cell phone rang. This time it was her best friend, Paula.

"Hey girl, how are you?" Alexis said.

"I'm good. So what's up?"

"The question is, what isn't?"

"Uh-oh. I had a feeling something was going on when you called me last night, and I'm sorry I couldn't talk."

"It wasn't a problem. I knew you and Rick had gone away for the holiday weekend, so I was just taking a chance on calling."

"We really had a great time. Chicago was wonderful, and we didn't even drive back until this morning."

"So you're off today?"

"I am. I called in, girl."

"Well, it's not like you ever miss work, even when you're sick, so good for you."

"But what's up?"

"My future mother-in-law."

"Oh boy. What did she do now?"

"You mean, what didn't she do."

Alexis filled Paula in on everything from Thanksgiving Day to what Geneva had said at the restaurant on Saturday to the way she'd shown her behind at church.

"Lex, I'm not even sure what to say, except...that woman is the devil!"

"Either that or she's secretly married to him. She literally hates me, and I've never done a thing to her."

"Well, you sort of did."

"Like what?"

"You met her son, the two of you fell in love, and now you're getting married."

"You'd think she'd be happy for him. If I had a son, and I knew he was happy and that he was marrying a woman who really loved him, I'd be thrilled. My heart would be content."

"Yeah, but not if you thought the way Mrs. Dupont does. She's the kind of woman who would never like any woman Chase was serious about."

"Well, she sure seems to love Renee, and they were serious at one time, too."

"Those are the key words: at one time. Because I'll bet everything I have that Mrs. Dupont didn't care all that much for her back then, either. She loves her now because she's out of the picture. Plus, she was probably putting on a show just to make you jealous."

"Maybe, but I'm tired of all her shenanigans. I'm a good person with a good heart, and I genuinely love her son. That's all that should matter."

"I think Chase should sit Mommy Dearest down for a little chat."

"That's what he's planning to do this evening."

"And for the love of God, when is she moving out? Why is she even still living there?"

"Chase says it's because she's lonely, but that she's promised to move out before the wedding."

"Yeah, right. The only way Mommy is moving is if Chase puts his foot down. If he doesn't tell her to leave, she's not going anywhere. I've seen this kind of thing before, so mark my word."

"I sure hope you're wrong, because I can't live with her. I *won't* live with her."

"It'll all work out. Chase just has to let her know what the deal is. Period."

"I hope he does," Alexis said. "Sooner rather than later."

Chapter 6

Oh my God," Alexis said out loud, as if someone were sitting in her home office listening to her. "I can't believe this is actually happening." Alexis had read the email from Tracey, her assistant, two times already, but she couldn't help reading the first sentence again: "They've agreed to pay you twenty thousand dollars."

It had been only last week that a representative from C&G Pharmaceuticals had contacted Tracey, asking if Alexis was available to speak at the company's sales conference next April. C&G was one of the largest corporations in the country, so Tracey had gotten back to them right away. She sent them Alexis's requested speaker's fee and travel expense requirements. It wasn't that Alexis hadn't believed they would sign her on to speak, but she'd half expected they would counter with a lower number. Now they wanted to confirm the date and draw up an agreement.

Alexis was so excited and very thankful, because this

would be the highest fee she'd been paid since becoming a motivational speaker. She had a feeling, though, that the superior recommendation from another large pharmaceutical company that she'd recently worked with had likely helped C&G make their decision. Tracey had learned during her initial communication with them that this was the reason they were contacting Alexis.

Alexis thought back over her life and all the careers she'd had, as well as about the scenic route she'd taken to get her associate's, bachelor's, and master's degrees. She even remembered how her first paid speaking engagement had earned her only one hundred dollars, but how proud she'd still been to receive it. Then, she'd eventually moved up to five hundred dollars, then to a thousand, and then to twenty-five hundred. But over the last two years, she'd gone from five to ten thousand to now twenty to speak at huge sales conferences. It was all such a great blessing from God, and it was Him whom she gave all the credit to.

As Alexis thought about how well her career was doing, she smiled with joy, but it wasn't long before she thought about her mom and how she wished she could tell her this good news in person. She knew her mom was with her in her heart, but Alexis would give anything to spend five minutes with her again. Two minutes, if that was all that was possible. Alexis always tried to be happy and go on with her life the way her mother had told her she wanted her to, but it was still very hard for her. Then, of course, when it came to the holiday season, she always hoped that things would be better and that at some point she'd be able to enjoy Christmas the same as the next person; but after five years, it still hadn't happened. And to this date, she'd never even purchased her own Christmas tree.

Before her mom had passed, Alexis hadn't seen a reason to buy one, because during the entire month of December she would drive straight to her mom's house when she finished working on the weekdays, and she would spend most of her time there on the weekends as well. But ever since then, Alexis had been too depressed to do decorating of any kind. She'd had no desire to so much as hang a beautiful wreath on her front door. There were times, however, when she wished she did have the desire to decorate, cook Christmas hors d'oeuvres, and play all her Christmas CDs, but that desire never progressed beyond a few thoughts. She wondered why she'd ordered both Kem's and Mary J. Blige's latest Christmas CDs as soon as they'd been released in October, yet they still sat on her kitchen island unopened. Alexis would have also liked to invite over friends and family members for a Christmas get-together one Saturday or Sunday in December, but she just didn't have it in her. The thought of it all was very painful, and no matter how much she considered the idea of celebrating, what she thought about more was the fact that her mom was no longer there.

There was at least one Christmas ritual she did keep, though: She bought Christmas gifts for everyone close to her. During the first or second week in December, she spent one day online ordering certain gifts, and she spent one day out at the mall purchasing the rest of them. Buying for others always gave her joy, even at other times of the year, so she sort of looked forward to those two particular days leading up to Christmas. She also gave lots of toy donations to a number of charities for kids, and she donated money to local food banks that handed out Christmas baskets. Still, she took care of every bit of that in those same two allotted days. Some years, she even sent out Christmas cards. But if she was feeling exceptionally sad, no cards went out at all, and she also didn't attend church the Sunday before Christmas, because she knew Christmas would be the focus of the entire service.

Alexis certainly didn't want to sound whiny or ungrateful, because she knew God had blessed her with good health, a wonderful fiancé, family and friends, and a great career, but she couldn't help the way she felt. She was also sure that some people basically thought she should move on and get over it. Those were likely people who hadn't lost a mother, or worse, people who *had* lost a mother but hadn't had a good relationship with her—or they'd had no relationship with their mother at all. So, clearly, none of those folks would ever understand or have any sympathy for someone like Alexis—not until they walked in her shoes.

But maybe the Christmas prayer she'd written last night before going to bed, the one Pastor Black had asked the congregation to write on Sunday, would help her.

Alexis pulled it up on her computer screen.

Dear Lord,

My prayer for this Christmas is that I will experience much joy and happiness during this entire holiday season. Losing my mom is the most painful experience I've ever suffered through, and it continues to be extremely difficult for me. Whether it be the loss of a mother, father, sibling, or other family member, the pain of losing a loved one is truly heartbreaking and very real. So, my prayer is that You will give me the love and desire I need to celebrate Christmas again. Not just this year, but also for each year hereafter. I pray that You will bless others who are hurting as well, and that You will eliminate all sadness and loneliness for them completely. Then, Father, while I recognize and fully honor Jesus's birthday, my prayer is that You will fill my heart with joy about Christmas as a whole. My prayer is that You will surround me with family members, friends, and even people I don't know who will help me through this very trying process. I pray for this and for all other blessings in Your Son Jesus's name, Amen.

When Alexis finished reading her prayer, she smiled. She truly hoped God would deliver her from sadness and loneliness just as she'd asked him to. Strangely enough, she actually felt a little better. Maybe it was because she had faith that God would in fact bring joy into her life and change the way she felt. She'd already tried other methods, such as joining a grief support group, talking with her pastor, and seeing a grief counselor, and although she had eventually started to feel better, November and December were still difficult months for her. She also wasn't sure why she felt fine on all the other holidays, such as Memorial Day, the Fourth of July, and Labor Day. But maybe it was because Thanksgiving and Christmas were the top two days for family get-togethers and to her, the idea of celebrating with family just wasn't the same. She did have her sister and niece and her mom's brothers and sisters, whom she loved dearly and would do anything for, but none of them could take the place of her mother. Her mom had been her mother, her sister, and her best friend all wrapped up in one, so how on earth could anyone ever fill those kinds of shoes? How could anyone love Alexis with the same genuine, unconditional love that her mom had given her? It just wasn't possible, and Alexis knew she had to somehow accept that and be okay with it.

As Alexis leaned back in her chair, her phone rang. It was her sister.

"Hey," Alexis said.

"Hey, how's it goin'?"

"Okay. What about you?"

Sabrina paused. "Not good."

"Why, what's wrong?"

"I need two hundred fifty dollars."

Alexis closed her eyes and gathered her composure, because it was always something when it came to Sabrina. Alexis should have known she needed money, because she rarely called for any other reason. She did this all the time.

"What do you need it for?" Alexis asked.

"Why do you always do that?" Sabrina spat. "It's not like you don't have it. The only thing that should matter, anyway, is that you know I'll pay you back."

"No, see, that's the problem. You almost never pay me back, and when you do I've had to ask you for it. Even then, you yell and curse like I don't even have a right to question you."

"Look, sis, I'm sorry. Can you do it or not?"

Sabrina apologizing? Now, that was a new one.

"I need to know why, and if you can't tell me, then so be it."

"Fine; if you must know, I need it to pay my electric bill. If I don't do it by the end of the day, they're gonna shut my lights off."

"What about Melvin?

"What about him?"

"Why can't he pay it? And why do you keep doing this?"

"Doing what, Alexis?"

"Spending beyond your means and taking care of a man who doesn't help you with anything. He works every single day, yet he spends his money elsewhere. Then on top of that, he's been living with you all these years, not to mention he's Courtney's father, but he still won't marry you."

"Well, *Miss Thing*, for the record, not everyone can snag some filthy rich CEO the way you have. And I would appreciate it if you would leave Melvin out of this."

"Sabrina, please. This has nothing to do with me. This is about you and the terrible choices you keep making. You have so much potential, and you could be doing so much better for yourself."

"Not everyone is as lucky as you. Some of us have to work for what we get."

"Oh, so now you think I don't work?"

"Not much. I mean, you travel around doing those speaking engagements, but that's certainly not work. Anybody can get up and talk to a bunch of people."

"You know what?" Alexis said, switching her phone to her other ear. "I'm gonna pretend you didn't just say that. But what I do wanna talk about is why you won't move out of a house that you can barely pay for. The rent is sky high, so why can't you move into an apartment where the expenses are a lot lower? Because if you did, maybe you'd be able to pay your bills on time."

Alexis waited for a response, but Sabrina hung up on her. Just like that. And all because she didn't want to hear anything Alexis had to say. What Sabrina wanted was for Alexis to give her the money and keep quiet. But Alexis wasn't going to give her a thing. At least that's what she'd decided before she caught sight of that email again, the one where C&G was offering her twenty thousand dollars. This, of course, made her feel guilty, and she definitely didn't want her twelve-year-old niece to sleep in a house with no lights. So she called Sabrina back.

"What's your ComEd account number?" was all Alexis said. "That way, I can just pay it by phone."

"Why can't you just give me the money, and let me pay my own bill?"

"Look. Take it or leave it, Sabrina."

Sabrina hung up on Alexis again. But within seconds, she texted over her account number.

If Alexis had been a cursing woman, she would have had a few choice words for Sabrina, but at the same time, she knew she'd be wasting her breath. With Sabrina, there was always drama, and it was never worth losing any sleep over. So instead, Alexis did what she always did. She came to Sabrina's rescue—for the kazillionth time. Mostly, she did it for the welfare of her niece.

Chapter 7

Chase strolled into The Tuxson, looking as handsome as ever, and removed his sunglasses. His light gray tailor-made suit looked as though it wouldn't wrinkle even if someone balled it up, and he wore the classiest shoes Alexis had seen on a man. She'd arrived about five minutes earlier and had been waiting for him in the lobby near the water fountain. She was glad to see him.

"Hey, baby," he said, hugging her and pecking her on the lips.

"Hey yourself."

"Looking as beautiful as always, I see."

"Why, thank you," she said, smiling. A few months ago, Chase had given her this stylish designer skirt suit for her birthday, and while it was a bit pricier than what she was willing to pay for any piece of clothing, she couldn't deny how much she loved it. Fuchsia was one of her favorite colors, and Chase had remembered that.

As they approached the same maître d' who'd seated

them for breakfast on Saturday, a group of men dressed in corporate attire walked toward them from the dining area. Alexis recognized a couple of them from Chase's office.

"Heading back?" Chase asked Frank, one of his VPs.

"We are."

"And I trust you gentlemen enjoyed your lunch?" Chase asked three other men Alexis hadn't seen before.

"We did. Frank and John are taking very good care of us."

"Glad to hear it. Oh, and please excuse my manners. This is Alexis, my fiancée. Honey, you know Frank and John, but this is Bob, David, and Gerard. Their company is one of our top suppliers."

"It's a pleasure meeting all of you," she said, shaking their hands.

They each responded and smiled at her, but then Bob looked at Chase. "No wonder you pushed us off on Frank and John. If I had a gorgeous woman like this, I'd do the same. Don't blame you at all."

They all laughed.

"I'll see you guys at the four o'clock meeting," Chase said.

"Enjoy your lunch," Bob said.

As the men left the restaurant, the maître d' led Chase and Alexis to a table for two by a window that overlooked the river. When he set their menus down and walked away, Alexis scanned her surroundings. After all these years, The Tuxson was still Mitchell's premier restaurant and *the* place to take anyone who came to town.

Alexis clasped her hands together and rested them on the table. "So how long will your suppliers be here?"

"Through tomorrow or Thursday. But for the most part, Frank and John and a couple of my directors are handling the entire visit. I normally spend quite a bit of time with them, but because we have a new aerospace product launching next week, I need to focus on that. Enough about me, though. We're here to celebrate that huge speaker's fee you've been offered. Baby, I am so proud of you, and this is only the beginning."

"It's pretty exciting, and I still can't believe it."

"Well, I believe it, and before you know it, you'll be earning the same as Bill and Hillary."

"Yeah, right. Six figures to speak for an hour or less? Please."

"Anything's possible with faith and hard work."

"True, but I never even thought I'd get to twenty thousand. I was just happy to get five and ten."

"I'm really happy for you, and so proud to be marrying a woman who has her own life and identity. It's a good feeling, and I really respect you for that. A lot of women I've dated couldn't have cared less about having a career or doing anything on their own. Mostly, they wanted to marry me because of the money I have. They wanted to shop and have babies. I don't mind a woman doing either of those things, and I even encourage it, but I still want a woman who knows who she is and who wants to have a life outside of her husband and children."

"I've always wanted to work for myself. From the time

I was a small girl, my mom told me that I should always be able to stand on my own two feet. And I've never forgotten that. Plus, in two years, I'll be forty, and it's like I've been saying to you all along, I'm not sure I wanna have any children. I'm also glad you don't have a problem with that."

"I really don't. My job requires a lot of hours and dedication, and there will certainly be times when you and I will both be traveling. So, if we have a child, I'll be happy, and if we don't, I'll still be happy. Because let's be honest, as much as I will love our child and I would want to be a full-time parent, you'll end up doing most of the work. Most mothers tend to do the majority of it when it comes to raising children, so I want you to make the final decision about that."

"You're such a thoughtful man, and that really means a lot, Chase."

Shortly after the waiter set their food in front of them, Chase and Alexis held hands while Chase said grace. But when they opened their eyes, Geneva and Renee, Chase's ex, were walking toward them.

Alexis wondered if anyone could see steam shooting from the top of her head. She wanted so badly to set Geneva straight. She wanted to call her everything but a child of God, yet she prayed for restraint.

Geneva touched Chase's shoulder. "Oh my. What a pleasant surprise. I knew you'd said you were taking Alexis to lunch, but I had no idea you were coming here."

It was right then and there that Alexis wanted to call

Geneva a flat-out liar. She knew good and well that when Chase was working, he usually came to The Tuxson for lunch. This was only the second time, but Alexis was already growing tired of Geneva's need to throw Renee in her face.

Chase just looked at his mother, but for the first time, Alexis could tell he wasn't happy with her. He knew she was trying to cause problems between them on purpose. Renee seemed to be enjoying the whole dirty scheme and basically couldn't keep her eyes off Chase. But finally, she and Geneva said their good-byes and went on their way.

Alexis stared at Chase with no smile and no words to speak.

"Baby, I don't know what to say. My mother never even liked Renee all that much when we were dating, so I can't imagine why she's spending time with her now."

Alexis thought about what Paula had said yesterday about Geneva only liking Renee now because she and Chase weren't together any longer.

"Chase, come on," Alexis said. "She's doing it because she doesn't like me. She doesn't want you to marry me, and she's trying her best to break us up."

"Well, that's not going to happen."

"I thought you were going to talk to her."

"I was, but I got home late and then I really didn't think about it anymore."

"Well, I wish you'd sit down with her, because things can't keep going like this. I know Geneva is your mom, but I won't continue being around someone who goes out of her way to disrespect me. I've never done anything to her except try to be nice."

"I know that, baby, and again, I'm really sorry."

"It's not your fault, but it is your responsibility to talk to her."

"I will. I just don't understand why Mother is doing this."

Alexis didn't bother repeating what she'd told him only a few seconds ago: that his mother didn't like her and she didn't want him to marry her. It was as simple as that, and when a mother didn't like her future or current daughter-in-law for no reason, there wasn't a whole lot that could be done about it. But again, Alexis wanted Chase to talk to his mother so that she would at least stop playing games and being rude to her.

Alexis gazed out the window, watching waves flowing down the river. Neither Chase nor she had spoken a word for the last five minutes. Finally, Alexis said, "I so wish my mom were here," but she never took her eyes off the water.

"I know, and I really wish I'd gotten a chance to meet her. It sounds like she was a wonderful woman."

"She was, and one of the things that made her so special was that she never tried to hurt other people. She always tried to say nice things or do nice things for others, even if she hardly knew them. She also had a big heart and a very forgiving one, and that meant everything."

"I realize this isn't a very happy time of year for you and that you don't like to celebrate, but I'm really hoping you'll spend Christmas Eve and Christmas Day with Mother and me and a few of our friends."

Alexis continued looking toward the river because Geneva was the last person she wanted to be around for two days straight. Geneva would surely find more ways to make Alexis miserable, and Alexis didn't want to deal with that. But she also didn't want Chase to spend Christmas without the woman he was marrying. It wasn't fair to him, and Alexis would do what she needed to do to be there for him."

"I would never spend such a special holiday without you," she said. "It will be hard for me, the same as always, but at least we'll be together."

Chase reached across the table and grabbed both of her hands. "Remember yesterday when I told you how much I love you?"

Alexis looked at him and nodded.

"Well, I hope you won't ever forget that. You truly are my everything, and I always want to be here for you. I also don't want to be like my father. Working day and night for years is what pretty much killed him, and I don't want that kind of life. I'm not saying I want to give up my position as CEO, because I don't, but what I do want is to be the kind of husband who has his priorities in order. God, you, my family, and then work. I don't want it to be the other way around."

"I love you, too, and I'm so glad God brought us together," she said, but she thought about Chase's father and what he'd just told her about him. He was never home, and maybe this was the reason Geneva was so clingy when it came to Chase. Maybe this was also the reason she didn't want him to get married. Alexis now felt a bit sorry for Geneva, and her heart softened toward her. Maybe what Alexis needed to do was sit down with her to let her know she wasn't trying to take her son away from her. Alexis had always felt that a mother-in-law should never feel as though she'd lost a son, but instead she should be happy to have gained a daughter.

Alexis smiled at Chase and knew what she had to do. Tomorrow morning, she would call Geneva to schedule a time to stop by to talk with her. After that, things would be fine between them, and Alexis and Chase could continue with their wedding plans in peace. Life would be better for all three of them.

Chapter 8

$\mathcal{A}$lexis drove up Chase's driveway and turned off her car. With as many times as she'd visited him, it was still hard to imagine that she would soon be living here. In only a few months to be exact. Chase's home was breathtaking, inside and out. From the light brown brick exterior to the massive landscaping design, it was everything a woman could want. Marrying a wealthy man and having an eight-thousand-square-foot home hadn't been a lifelong dream of hers, yet for some reason, God had seen fit to give it to her. Unlike a lot of young girls who grew up fantasizing about the day they would marry their Prince Charming—specifically a rich one—Alexis had only wanted to graduate from college, find a husband who loved her unconditionally, and have a successful career she could be proud of. There was no doubt that Chase was in fact the man of her dreams, but she would have fallen in love with him even if he'd been her mailman. For all she cared, he could have earned minimum wage, working anywhere, as long as he loved her, spent quality time with her, and protected her.

Alexis stepped out of the car, walked up the winding sidewalk, and rang the doorbell. Two large Christmas wreaths hung on either side of the double doors, and they were adorned with red and green silk ribbon. Margaret opened the door almost immediately. She was Chase's housekeeper, and although she didn't live there, she cooked meals, cleaned, and washed clothes for Chase and his mother five days a week.

"Good morning, Miss Fletcher. Please come in," Margaret said, standing slightly behind the wooden door.

Alexis stepped inside the white marble entryway. "Thank you, and how are you today Margaret?"

"I'm doing well."

Margaret showed Alexis into the living room. Shortly after, Geneva walked in but didn't speak. She wore yet another expensive knit suit, and Alexis had learned a long time ago that Geneva dressed this way daily, even if she had nowhere special to go. Alexis, on the other hand, had on an off-white cashmere turtleneck sweater and jeans.

Geneva narrowed her eyes at Margaret. "Why are you just standing there?"

"I'm sorry ma'am. I just wanted to make sure you didn't need anything."

"If I did I would have already informed you. What I want is for you to get going so you can get back here. You have a lot of work to do this afternoon."

"Yes, ma'am. I won't be long," she said, turning and

leaving and Alexis could see how afraid of Geneva Margaret was.

"We can chat over here," Geneva said to Alexis.

Ceramic cups and croissants sat on the marble-topped wooden table that separated two white leather high-back chairs. Alexis couldn't help noticing the mega-tall Christmas tree, that was very tastefully decorated in traditional red and green, that stood in the corner. It was only the first week of December, yet several gifts were already stacked under it.

"Please have a seat," Geneva told her. "I'm sorry Margaret won't be here to serve refreshments, but I needed her to run some important errands. Would you like a cup of tea? Croissant, maybe?"

"No, thank you. I'm fine."

Geneva crossed her legs. "Figures."

"Excuse me?"

"Nothing. So, what did you want to see me about?"

"Us, and how we seem to have gotten off to a really bad start."

Geneva stared at her. "I guess I don't know what you mean."

"Can I be honest?"

"Go ahead."

"It's pretty obvious that you don't like me very much, and I'm not sure why. I mean, I know you and Chase are very close, and I just hope you don't think I'm trying to interfere with that."

Geneva raised her eyebrows and quietly laughed.

"You've got to be kidding. Honey, you give yourself way too much credit. You could never come between my son and me."

"But that's what I'm saying," Alexis went on to explain. "I would never try to. I love Chase, Chase loves me, and I really want you and me to get to know each other better."

"Hmmph, well, maybe it's time for me to be honest."

"I would appreciate that, so please do."

"I'm not going to beat around the bush. I don't like you because you're simply not good enough to marry my son. Chase's father and I raised him in a very high-class, well-cultured household, and we always had a certain kind of wife in mind for him. Don't get me wrong, I know you earn a few dollars from your little speaking business or from whatever it is you do, but you weren't born into money the way Chase was. You haven't a clue about the wealthy lifestyle Chase is used to living. I doubt you've served on even one foundation board or hosted a single charity ball," she said, eyeing Alexis up and down from head to toe. "And you certainly don't dress like the wife of a CEO. You don't even have the right kind of wardrobe to go with that massive ring Chase gave you."

Alexis was stunned. Here she'd put forth an effort to try to make things right between her and Geneva, yet all Geneva had done was cut her down with insults. Alexis had known all along that Geneva didn't like her, but she'd had no idea she thought so lowly of her as a person.

Money and status weren't everything, but clearly they meant the world to Geneva.

Alexis didn't say anything, however, Geneva continued.

"So, don't you think you should just forget about these ridiculous wedding plans of yours? I mean, you do keep saying you love him, right?"

"I do love him," Alexis said matter-of-factly. "So, why would I forget about anything?"

"Because if you love him, then I'm sure you want what's best for him. If you break off the engagement, he'll have a chance to marry a woman who's right for him."

"Like who, Geneva? Renee?"

"Maybe. Or someone else, even. I just want my son to be happy and well taken care of. I want him to have the right kind of woman on his arm when he's entertaining his business associates. When he's invited to the many social events we attend throughout the year. Or what about his friends from Yale? You won't even know how to handle yourself around those kinds of people. You didn't attend an Ivy League school the way Chase did."

"Chase doesn't seem to mind that I didn't come from money. He loves me for who I am."

"That's because love is blind, and he doesn't know any better. Sometimes sex can confuse a man."

Alexis frowned. "Not that it's any of your business, but we don't have sex. We're waiting until we get married."

"But you had sex a few times when you first met."

Alexis scrunched her forehead, completely mortified. "He told you that?"

"Of course not. But as soon as he started seeing you, he also started spending nights away from home, and that's when I checked his dresser drawer. I noticed one condom missing after another."

"You actually go through his personal belongings? Does he know that?"

"No, but if you told him he wouldn't be shocked. Chase knows who I am. Plus, I'm his mother, and mothers have a right to know anything they want about their children. And anyway, what woman teases a man with sex for a few months but then cuts him off as soon as he proposes to her? What sense does that make?"

"I've always known that having sex before marriage is wrong, but I'm not perfect, Geneva. Chase and I fornicated, but we both agreed to stop."

Geneva pursed her lips. "Like I said, I want my son to marry the right kind of woman, and unfortunately, dear, that just isn't you."

Alexis felt her heart racing. "I'm sorry you feel this way, and I think I should go now."

"No reason to rush off," Geneva said, smirking. "You just got here."

Alexis didn't even bother responding. Instead, she got to her feet, went down the hallway, and walked out the front door. She'd never felt more humiliated in her life. Geneva was a true piece of work, worse than some of the terrible mothers-in-law she'd heard about from friends and colleagues, and if Alexis had it her way, she would never see or speak to Geneva again. She also had to rethink her engagement to Chase, because it was clear that he and his mother came as a package deal. Once Alexis married Chase there would be no getting rid of her, and she would make Alexis's life a living hell. As it was, the woman was searching through her forty-year-old son's condoms and counting them. Who did that kind of thing? What kind of sick mother was Geneva? Nonetheless, she was far too much for Alexis to deal with, and marrying Chase might end up being the biggest mistake she'd ever make. She loved Chase, but sometimes love just wasn't enough. Sometimes common sense outweighed everything.

Chapter 9

Paula took a long swig of her lemonade and ate some of her cheese fries. "Girl, if you ask me, somebody needs to teach that witch a lesson."

She and Alexis were sitting at Riverside Deli, their usual meeting place for lunch. It had been only a couple of hours since Alexis's meeting with Geneva, and Paula was angrier than she was.

"The whole thing turned out to be a total disaster," Alexis said. "I'm not sure what I expected, but I definitely didn't expect her to be so mean. She treated me like I was beneath her and Chase, and like I would never fit in."

"I know one thing. I wouldn't let her bother me, and I certainly wouldn't let her ruin my relationship with a man who loves me."

Alexis took a bite of her tuna sandwich. "I agree, but only to a certain extent. I've heard way too much about these kinds of situations. It wouldn't be so bad if Chase stood up to his mother, but he won't. He really thinks she's moving out before the wedding, and that she and I are going to be close. He's being so naïve. Either that or he's in denial."

"That may be true, but if I were you, I would tell Chase everything that happened today. Everything his mother said. Especially the part about her counting his condoms. What a control freak."

"I do wanna tell him, but I also don't wanna seem like I'm trying to come between him and his mother. That's the same thing I tried to tell her."

"So then, if you decide to break things off, what excuse are you gonna give him?"

"I don't know."

"You have to tell him the truth, Lex. Even if he doesn't believe it or want to hear it, you have to be honest with him."

"I'll see. I just have to think about it."

"Well, if I haven't learned anything else, I have learned one thing," Paula said.

"What's that?"

"Beware of future mothers-in-law."

They both laughed. "Isn't that the truth," Alexis said.

"Although, from what I can tell, Rick's mom is a real sweetheart. She lives in Michigan, so I've only met her once, but she was very nice to me. As a matter of fact, when she came here, she and I spent hours at the mall and left Rick at home."

"I remember that."

Paula clasped her hands toward her chin and leaned forward. "And guess what else?"

"What?"

"I think Rick is gonna ask me to marry him."

"Get out of here! How wonderful, girl!"

"I know, right? He's been talking about how he's ready to settle down, and one day I saw him looking at rings online. When I walked in the room, though, he hurried and clicked away from the screen."

"He's the one," Alexis said. "I knew it from the first time I saw you guys together. You're perfect for each other."

Paula smiled again but didn't say anything.

Alexis squinted her eyes. "Don't tell me you're pregnant."

Paula cracked up laughing. "Girl, of course not. But I am up for a promotion to management."

"You're just full of great news today, aren't you? Congratulations. You so deserve this."

"It's been a long time coming, but I've worked my behind off for five years. Remember when I started out in that awful sales assistant job? I was so grateful to move up to claims adjuster and then supervisor. I'm sure getting my degree made all the difference for this latest promotion, though."

"I'm sure it did, and I'm so glad you decided to go back to school. It's never too late, and I just wish a lot of other people realized that. Whether you're eighteen or eighty, there's still time to better yourself."

"Yes indeed, but I won't lie. Starting college for the first time at thirty-three was scary. Especially since I had to work full-time and attend classes at night and online."

"Fear is normal, but I'm glad you didn't let it stop you. God gave you everything you needed, and now look at the reward."

Tears filled Paula's eyes. "I know, and thank you for always supporting me, Lex. Whenever I felt like giving up, it was you who kept encouraging me to keep going. You kept telling me I could do it, and I needed to hear that."

"You know I love you, and I'll always be in your corner."

"I also owe you for buying most of my books, and I haven't forgotten that."

"You don't owe me anything."

"But I do."

"Like I said, you don't owe me anything."

"But—"

"But nothing," Alexis said, laughing because they always playfully argued about this kind of thing. Alexis truly didn't want any payback, though, because she was just happy her best friend was moving up to management. She was as happy as if it had happened to her.

Paula ate more of her fries and drank more lemonade. "And hey, didn't you say we need to meet with the wedding planner again next month?"

"Yeah, but first we need to make sure there's actually going to be a wedding."

"There will be. You just have to handle this Geneva situation."

When Alexis heard her phone vibrating, she pulled it out of her purse. It was Chase calling.

She looked at Paula, took a deep breath, and answered. "Hey."

"What in the world did you say to my mother, Alexis?" His tone was curt and louder than normal.

"What do you mean?"

"Did you go by there?"

"Yes."

"Why?"

"Because I wanted to talk to her."

"Well, from the sound of it, you did a lot more than that."

"Excuse me?"

"My mother was crying her eyes out. She said you screamed and yelled at her like a madwoman and then you called her every kind of name you could think of. She said you told her you wanted her out of my house by the end of the week."

"What? I never said anything like that."

"She also said you threw a vase at her, and it crashed across the living room floor."

"Oh—my—God! And you believe her?"

"I don't know what to believe."

"Oh, so it's like that? Well, I bet you'll believe this!" she said, pressing the End button and tossing her phone onto the table.

"What was that all about?" Paula asked.

"Geneva called and told him a bunch of lies."

"What did she say?"

"That I threw a vase at her, told her to get out...you name it."

"What an evil witch. You're not gonna let her get away with this, are you?"

"I just wanna be done with all of it."

Alexis's phone vibrated again. It was Chase calling back, and she picked it up right away. "Look, Chase, why don't we just end this?"

"Is that what you want?"

"If you were so quick to believe your mother, then that means you're calling me a liar."

"No, I never said that, and I'm sorry I yelled at you. But my mother was really upset."

"I thought I was doing the right thing by going to talk to her, but now I regret it."

"Why couldn't you just wait for me to do it?"

"None of that matters now, because if nothing else, I finally know the truth about your mother and how she feels about me. She said some of the nastiest things, and she meant every word."

"I just don't understand why she would be so cruel or why she would call me with such an outlandish story."

"So you're still trying to say I'm lying?"

"No, I'm not. Look, we're both upset, so why don't we take the afternoon to cool down and then I'll stop by when I leave work."

"Whatever."

"See you then."

Alexis set her phone on the table again. She was livid and had a mind to call Geneva, but for all she knew, Geneva might make up more lies than she had already. This whole mess was completely out of control, and now Alexis thought more about ending everything. She wondered if it was best to leave well enough alone and move on. For good.

Chapter 10

What a day. As soon as Alexis had gotten home from having lunch with Paula, she'd taken off her sweater and jeans and slipped on a velour sweat suit. Come to think of it, it was her jeans and sweater that had caused Geneva to eye her up and down and then blurt out the words, "And you certainly don't dress like the wife of a CEO." Alexis had left there in such a hurry and had been so upset that she hadn't thought much about it then, but now she knew that there was nothing about her that Geneva approved of. Yes, Alexis had been raised up on the west side of Mitchell by two parents who'd finished high school and had then gone to work in factories, and yes, she'd gone to public school from kindergarten through twelfth grade and hadn't gone to any Ivy League school for college, yet that didn't mean she was any less of a person than Geneva or Chase. Her parents had still given her a good home, they'd earned a good living, and she'd never gone without anything she needed. They hadn't been wealthy by any stretch of the imagination, but they'd enjoyed a normal, happy Midwestern life, and Alexis didn't have any complaints. She wondered if Geneva could say the same, especially since, according to Chase, her husband had worked hours on end and never spent much time with them. Sure, Geneva had been able to shop and buy whatever she wanted, regardless of the cost, but did she truly know what it was like to be happily married? What Alexis wanted to know was whether she had ever known what it was like to just wake up happy, period. Alexis had experienced a lot of sadness, on and off, over the last five years; however, it was only because she'd lost her mother. Outside of that, she'd lived a pretty joyful life. She also had to go back to the fact that she was a good person with a good heart, so why wasn't that enough for Geneva? Why wasn't Alexis's undying love for Chase enough to qualify her as an ideal wife for him?

Alexis sat on the navy-blue leather sofa in her family room, drew her knees closer to her chest, and pulled the blanket closer to her neck. She turned on her television and examined the interior of her house. It wasn't even close to the size of Chase's home, but three thousand square feet was more than enough for one person, and she was content with it. She also had a very spacious kitchen, a living room, a dining room, and four bedrooms, one of which she'd turned into her office and one she'd made into a den. Of course, if for some reason Geneva were to ever come by there, she would likely laugh herself silly. She would feel sorry for Alexis for having to live in such a paltry manner.

Just as Alexis turned to Lifetime Movie Network, her doorbell rang. She knew it was Chase, because he'd called to say he was on his way, but normally he used his key and came right in. Alexis got up and opened the door for him.

"Hey," she said, waiting for him to kiss her the way he usually did. But instead, he walked past her, down the hall and into the family room. She followed behind him and climbed back onto the sofa with her blanket. Chase sat down in one of the chairs.

"So how are you?" he asked.

"How do you think, Chase?"

"I just don't understand why all this is happening. One minute you tell me to talk to my mother, and the next you're secretly driving over to talk to her yourself."

"So you think I sneaked over there behind your back? I'm not a child, Chase."

"No, but it just seems that you would have mentioned it to me. We talked on the phone this morning just like we always do."

"I guess I was hoping that me and your mother could work things out on our own. If I had it to do again, though, I would have stayed in my lane and left her alone."

"I wish you would have."

Alexis raised her eyebrows. "Why is it that you seem to be blaming me for all of this? You heard the way your mother talked to me at breakfast on Saturday. Then, how about the way she's suddenly parading Renee in front of me? You weren't even happy about that yourself."

"I know that, but how would you feel if your mother called you right now, crying and then insisting that someone had tried to attack her?"

Alexis stared at him with no emotion. "In case you've forgotten, my mother is gone. So I guess I'll never know, now will I?"

"Baby, I'm sorry," he said, scooting to the edge of the chair. "I didn't mean it that way. I was just trying to make a point. I was trying to get you to understand why I feel the way I do."

"There's nothing for me to understand. I told you what happened, and your mother is lying. And anyway, what did Margaret say? Did you ask her about me screaming at your mother, and breaking a vase across the floor?"

As soon as Alexis finished her last sentence, everything made sense. She'd just remembered that Margaret hadn't been there most of the time. Geneva hadn't wanted anyone to witness what she was up to.

"Margaret was out running errands," he said.

"Yeah, and don't you think that's pretty convenient?"

"What, you think my mother sent her out on purpose?"

"I told her what time I was coming over, and it's awfully strange that this just so happened to be the morning your mother needed Margaret to go places for her. Even I know that after Margaret cooks breakfast for you and your mother, she changes the sheets, washes clothes, and cleans the house. She does that until early afternoon when it's time to start dinner. She also doesn't run any errands until the afternoon either."

Chase took a deep breath and leaned back in the chair.

"Did you ask Margaret why she had to run errands so early?" Alexis asked.

"I haven't seen her. I stopped at home to check on Mother, and then I came straight over here. Margaret was already gone for the day."

"It's not like you don't have her phone number. So why not just call her?"

Chase glanced over at the television.

"Deep down, I think you know I'm telling the truth. You just don't wanna side with me over your mother. Which is fine, but don't expect me to keep taking this."

"There has to be some sort of way to work this out."

"There is."

"I'm listening."

"You have to set your mother straight. I'm not telling you to disrespect her, but you have to let her know that there's nothing she can do to break us up. Then you have to tell her it's time she move back home. Not just before the wedding, but by the end of this year."

"That's only a month from now," he said.

Alexis lowered her feet to the floor. "Look, Chase. If you don't feel comfortable with that, I will completely understand. But know that we can't be together."

"So you're making me choose between you and my mother?"

"No, I'm just telling you that I can't tolerate her anymore. I love you, but if you can't stand up to your mother now, you'll never do it when we're married, either. You'll never defend me, and your mother will say and do whatever she wants to me and get away with it."

Chase pulled off his suit jacket, removed his tie, and opened the first couple of buttons on his shirt. He walked over and sat on the edge of the sofa facing Alexis.

"Baby, I hate to admit this, but I feel like some sheltered child. I feel like I'm being pulled in two different directions."

"I'm sure you do, but Chase, look at me," she said, holding either side of his face. "I would never lie to you. Your mother told me that the reason she doesn't like me is because I'm not good enough for you. She said that if I loved you, I would walk away so you can marry a woman who's right for you. Do you wanna hear more?"

"I just don't understand why she would do something like this. And then that crazy story she told me."

Alexis couldn't tell if he was saying he now knew his mother was lying, or if he still believed she wasn't capable of going this far.

"Maybe we need to step back," she said. "After all, you've been with your mother all your life, and you've only known me for barely a year."

"That's not what I want."

"Well, we can't go on like this."

"What if the three of us sit down together?"

"That's fine, but are you going to tell your mother she has to move out?"

"Eventually."

"When?"

"Soon."

Alexis didn't believe him, but she also wasn't going to try to force him to kick his own mother out of his house. If Chase told his mother to leave only because Alexis wanted him to, he would always resent her for it, which meant they'd still be starting out their marital life with problems and animosity.

Chase pecked her on the lips. "Baby, can we go lie down and just hold each other? I'm so exhausted."

"Don't you think we need to settle things first?"

"I just can't talk about this anymore. We'll deal with it tomorrow."

Alexis gazed into his eyes.

"Baby, please," he said. "I just wanna rest my mind and be near you."

Alexis wasn't sure what to do at this point. Her heart declared one thing, yet her mind whispered another. She didn't want to end their engagement, but Geneva was a real hell-raiser who crafted real schemes, and she was good at it. She was the kind of woman who was willing to do whatever became necessary to get what she wanted.

But like Chase, Alexis was exhausted, physically and emotionally, and she didn't want to spend the rest of her evening discussing his mother. She didn't want to think about that woman at all.

Chapter 11

Alexis thought she heard Chase's phone ringing, but she didn't move. When it rang a third time, he reached over to the nightstand and picked it up. Alexis couldn't believe his mother was calling yet again. As it was, she'd already called his phone no less than four times after they'd laid down, and now here it was well after midnight.

"Hello?" he said, clearing his voice and trying to sound alert. "What?...When?...Which hospital?...I'm on my way."

Chase set his phone down and got up. "My mother's being rushed to the emergency room."

"Why, what happened?"

"I'm not sure."

"Do you want me to go with you?"

"Do you mind?"

"No," she said, pushing the covers back and getting to her feet. There was no doubt that Geneva wouldn't want her there, but she was going anyway to support Chase. Alexis also couldn't help wondering if this was another one of Geneva's tricks. Knowing her, there was nothing wrong at all and she was simply trying to find another way to gain Chase's sympathy. Thankfully, they'd fallen asleep fully dressed, so all Alexis had to do was slip on her socks and gym shoes. Chase sat in the chair in the corner, putting on his shoes, and then went into the living room and pulled on his blazer. They were out the door in no time.

When they arrived at the hospital, they left the car and rushed inside the ER entrance. Alexis hurried behind Chase as though she truly wanted to be there, but she wasn't happy. During the ride over, she'd asked him who'd called to tell him about his mother, and he'd told her it was Renee. Alexis had been livid, but she hadn't made anything of it because she knew Chase was worried about Geneva.

Chase moved closer to the admitting desk. "I'm here to see my mother, Geneva Dupont."

The clerk checked her computer and then said, "She's been taken to an examination room. I'll buzz you back there."

Chase and Alexis opened the door to the left of the reception window and one of the nurses escorted them to Geneva's room. Chase opened the door, and they walked in. Renee was sitting at her bedside, and it was all Alexis could do not to turn and leave.

Geneva reached out her arms, and the top of one of her

hands had an IV needle inserted in it. "I'm so glad you came, son. I was so afraid," she said, now crying.

Chase leaned down and hugged her. "Mother, what happened?"

"I don't know. Out of nowhere I became nauseated, and my head started pounding. The pain was excruciating, and then I felt dizzy. I thought I might be having a stroke," she said, and then glanced over at Chase's ex. "But thank God I called Renee, because had she not insisted I call 911, there's no telling what might've happened."

"Why didn't you call me?" he asked.

"Well, when I'd called earlier, you'd sounded like you were sleeping, so I didn't want to bother you again."

Boy, she was good. Alexis watched Geneva perform with great talent. She knew exactly what to say and how to say it, and Chase was already buying her story. Alexis didn't believe a word of it.

"Thank you so much for being here, son."

"Where else would I be?" he said. "And how are you feeling now?"

"I'm a lot better. Still not completely out of the woods, but much better since they gave me something for the pain and nausea. They're also going to take me down for an MRI."

Just then, a radiology technician knocked on the door and opened it. "Geneva Dupont?" she said.

"Yes?"

"I'm Jessica, and I'm here to take you to our X-ray department."

"Okay," Geneva said.

"How long do you think it'll be?" Chase asked.

The technician walked behind Geneva's bed and released the security latches near the wheels. "Maybe a half hour or so."

"Then, Mother, we'll just wait for you here."

"That's fine, son."

As Jessica rolled her out, Geneva looked at Renee, displaying the most pitiful look Alexis had ever seen, but interestingly enough, she hadn't glanced at Alexis the whole time she'd been there. She pretended that only Chase and Renee were in the room with her, and Alexis was ready to leave there.

Chase closed the door, and the room fell into awkward silence. Renee gazed up at the TV, acting as though she were watching whatever was on, and Chase seemed out of sorts as well. There weren't any other seats, so Alexis turned toward the door and said, "I'm going back out to the waiting area."

But to her surprise, Renee said, "That's probably a good idea."

Alexis quickly turned back around. "Are you talking to me?"

"Yeah, I am. Geneva told me how you attacked her, so you've got a lot of nerve showing up here. The way you treated her was so uncalled for, and it's probably the reason she's ill."

Alexis folded her arms. "Why are you even here yourself, Renee? And for the record, I never did anything to Geneva."

"I'm here because I care about her. Geneva is very special to me."

"Baby, let's just go," Chase said, opening the door.

Alexis walked ahead of him, and when they returned to the waiting area, she dropped down in a chair and tossed her handbag to the right of her. Chase sat next to her on the other side.

She folded her arms. "How long do you expect me to keep putting up with this?"

Chase leaned his head against the wall and took a deep breath.

"So you're not going to say anything?" she asked.

"Baby, look. I don't like the fact that Renee is here, either, but right now I just wanna make sure Mother is okay. See what her test results are."

"I understand that, but I also think you should ask Renee to leave."

"You know I don't like a lot of conflict, so why don't you just ignore her? That's what I'm doing."

Alexis stared at him and then pulled out her cell phone.

Chase watched her. "What are you doing?"

"Calling a taxi."

"Lexi, please don't do this."

"I told you I won't keep being disrespected this way, but apparently you're not hearing me."

"I do hear you, and I understand what you're saying, but I also have to wait for my mother."

Alexis stood up. "You do what you need to, but I'm out of here."

"Just like that? Even though you know how worried I am?"

"It's not like you're here alone. Renee would love to sit with you and console you."

"Now you're just being ridiculous."

"Am I? Well, like I said, I'm out of here."

As Alexis walked away from him, she Googled local cab companies and dialed the first one she saw. It didn't take more than ten minutes for a taxi to pick her up. It took even less time for her to make a decision about Chase. She was calling off the wedding and giving him his ring back. All this Geneva drama just wasn't worth it, and it was time Alexis wised up and faced facts. This whole relationship had been too good to be true since the very beginning. She hadn't wanted to think that, but now she knew the truth: Fairy tales just didn't happen.

Chapter 12

When Alexis heard her phone ringing, she looked away from her computer to see who it was. When she saw Chase's number, she hit Ignore. He was calling bright and early, but since he hadn't bothered to call when she left the hospital last night, she didn't have much to say to him.

She clicked her Microsoft Word icon and pulled up the speech she'd been working on before Thanksgiving. It was for a university speaking engagement she had the second week of January, but she always tried to finish writing her speeches at least six weeks ahead of time. That way, she had time to review them and make any necessary changes. Normally, when she was asked to focus on time management, it was for various sales forces throughout the country, but it was always nice when she was able to gear her talks toward time management for college students. She loved speaking to any group, but when she spoke to young men and women it felt a bit more rewarding because they were highly ambitious and they believed the sky was the limit. This made Alexis feel as though she was helping to prepare them for life after graduation, at least in some small way.

Alexis typed a few lines of her speech, went back and made some changes toward the beginning, and looked over at her cell phone. Chase was calling her again. If she didn't answer, he would likely call a third time, so she picked it up.

"Hello?"

"How are you?" he asked.

"Good."

"Are you working?"

"Yep."

"So I guess you're still upset."

"Nope."

"You're not upset, but you're giving me all these one-word answers?"

Alexis leaned back in her chair. "What is it you want, Chase?"

"To talk to you."

"About what?"

"Last night. I know you weren't happy about Renee being there, but that wasn't my fault."

"Yeah, but you should have asked her to leave."

"I didn't invite her."

"But you knew it made me uncomfortable, and you should've handled it. You also knew your mother called Renee on purpose."

"Whether she did or didn't, I brought *you* to the hospital, and that's who I wanted to be there with me."

Alexis heard him, but her feelings about Renee being there hadn't changed. Now she wanted to know about Geneva's diagnosis. "So, what was wrong with your mother? Did they find out anything?"

"Not yet."

Alexis wanted to laugh out loud. "Did they admit her?"

"No, they released her around four a.m., but they want her to follow up with our family physician."

"Did Renee stay the whole time?"

"Yes, but I never said one word to her."

Alexis didn't say anything else.

"Why are you so upset about this?"

"Wouldn't you be?"

"About what? Some man you broke up with and don't care anything about? No, that wouldn't bother me at all."

"Well, this is about more than just Renee. It's about your mother and how she's never going to stop trying to cause trouble for us. She wants me out of your life, and now she's faking stroke symptoms to get your attention?"

"I don't think my mother would pretend about something like this. She's capable of a lot of things, but not something this serious."

Alexis raised her eyebrows. "Chase, your mother is capable of that and then some. You just can't see it because you love her. Your mother is very slick with her schemes, and she knows how to manipulate you. My guess is that she's been doing it for years."

"But she's still my mother, and you can't expect me to just cut her off."

"I never asked you to. All I wanted was for you to talk to her, but you couldn't even do that. You act like you're afraid of her."

"No, but I do love her, and I respect her."

"Well, I can't deal with this anymore."

"And what does that mean exactly?"

"Our engagement is off."

"You're breaking up with me because of my mother?"

"I'm ending things because as long as your mother is around, we'll never be happy."

"I'm not sure what you expect me to do. I mean, I've told you how much I love you and that I want to spend the rest of my life with you, but that's not enough?"

"No. It's not."

"Then you must not have loved me the way you claimed," he said.

"I did love you. I still do. But I won't tolerate a meddling mother-in-law who doesn't think I'm good enough. I won't be talked down to or have ex-girlfriends paraded around me like they're family members."

"I can't control who my mother sees or talks to."

"That's fine, Chase, but let's just end this, okay?"

"Fine, if that's what you want."

"I do."

"Then I guess there's nothing else to say."

"I guess not. You take care," she said, and hung up.

She exhaled and swallowed back tears. She refused to cry about this, because crying wasn't going to help anything. Not to mention, she'd cried enough over the last couple of weeks. It was time she shook off her pain and frustration and got her life back on track.

She sat in front of her computer, unable to work any longer, but just as she prepared to head into the kitchen to get something to drink, her phone rang again. Why wouldn't Chase just leave her alone? She loved him, God knew she did, but marriage wasn't going to work for them. As she moved closer to her phone, though, she saw that it was her niece, Courtney, and felt relieved.

"Hey, sweetie. How are you?"

"Aunt Lexi, can you come get me?"

"Why? Aren't you feeling well? Are you at school?"

"No, I'm home. It's too cold to take a shower, and my feet and hands are almost frozen."

"Why? And where is your mom?"

"She and my dad already left for work, but our gas got turned off on Friday and we don't have any heat."

"What?"

"We have a couple of space heaters, but they're not really helping. I mean, I'm fine if I sit right in front of the bigger one, but I just can't take any more cold showers. I'm so cold, Aunt Lexi."

"You just get dressed and pack a bag. I'm on my way."

Chapter 13

Honey, I am so sorry you had to go through this," Alexis said, hugging her niece. As promised, she'd rushed across town to pick up Courtney, and as soon as she'd gotten her back to her house, Courtney had taken a hot shower and slipped on a pair of flannel pajamas and some socks. She'd still seemed to have chills every now and then, though, so Alexis had given her one of her terry cloth robes to put on.

"I really wish you would have called me right away on Friday," Alexis continued while sitting on the opposite end of the sofa from her niece. "You know I'm always here for you, and you can call me about anything. That's why I got you a cell phone."

"I know," Courtney said, nestling her long, thin body into the corner of the couch with a blanket. "But my mom told me not to. She said if I did, I'd be on punishment. But I couldn't help it, Aunt Lexi. I couldn't keep being cold like that."

"Of course you couldn't, and don't you feel bad about calling me. I'll deal with your mom."

"Aunt Lexi?" Courtney said with teary eyes.

"Yeah?"

"Can I come live with you?"

"Well, honey, you know I wouldn't mind, but we'd have to clear that with your mom."

"She'll never let me move. You'll have to take her to court and make her."

"Courtney, is the heat being turned off the only thing going on, or is there something else?"

"We never have any food, and my mom and dad argue all the time. My dad stays out really late, then he comes home drunk and they scream at each other for hours. I can't sleep when they do that, and last week I got in trouble at school for sleeping in class. I also failed my math test."

Alexis was horrified. "Sweetie, I had no idea."

"But please don't tell my mom I told you. She'll be so mad."

"I know you're afraid, but I at least have to talk to her about keeping you up all night. You can't keep living like that or keep getting bad grades. And what is it that they're arguing about?"

"My dad and all the women he messes around with. She also accuses him of being on that stuff."

Now Alexis was sorry she'd asked. She wasn't sure what she'd expected to hear, but it hadn't been any of this. The last thing she wanted was to have her twelve-year-old niece discussing drugs or women, especially when it had to do with her own father.

"Can I stay with you?" Courtney asked again.

"We'll have to talk to your mom."

"She really is gonna be so mad at me."

"You just let me handle things. I'll call her when she gets off work."

After Alexis made Courtney breakfast, Courtney laid back on the sofa and fell asleep. When she'd woken up, Alexis had fixed her a late lunch, and she'd fallen asleep again. That had been four hours ago, and Alexis was so through with her sister. Sabrina had never been responsible and had never fully taken care of Courtney the way she should have, but forcing a child to live without heat during the first week of December in Illinois was just plain reckless. Then, to hear that Courtney didn't always have food to eat had infuriated her even more. She had a mind to report Sabrina to the proper authorities, and if Sabrina hadn't been her sister she would have. Still, she wouldn't simply ignore what was going on, either, and she was planning to do something about it.

Alexis picked up her phone to call Paula, but when she did, Courtney walked into her office.

"My mom just called my phone, and she's on her way over here. She was really mad, and she said I'm gonna get it."

Alexis stood up and wrapped her arm around Courtney. "Don't worry. Everything's gonna be fine. You'll see."

They sat in the living room, waiting, and sure enough the doorbell rang. Alexis got up, ready for battle.

As soon as she opened the door, Sabrina and her no-good boyfriend, Melvin, waltzed in, yelling.

"You've got a lot of nerve," Sabrina said to Alexis. "Taking my child and bringing her over here without telling anybody."

"What did you expect me to do, Sabrina? Leave her in the cold? Let her starve?"

Sabrina squinted her eyes at her. "Look, Alexis. Courtney is *my* child, not yours, and if you ever take her without my permission again, I'll have you arrested."

"And if you ever force my niece to sleep in the cold and go without eating again, I'm calling Child Protective Services."

"That's why I never liked you," Melvin said, brushing past her. "Always up in somebody's business. Always tryin' to play mommy to somebody else's child." He walked over to Courtney. "You go get your things so we can get out of here."

Sabrina pulled her purse farther up on her shoulder. "Yeah, go get your stuff right now, Courtney! I told you good not to call your aunt, but you did it anyway, and now I'm takin' that phone of yours."

"You're not taking anything," Alexis said matter-of-factly. "I bought Courtney that phone, remember? I buy all her clothes and anything else she needs, too."

"Courtney, give your aunt her phone," Melvin said. "Give her that funky little phone so we can be done with her. No one asked you to buy that phone for her, anyway."

Alexis folded her arms, struggling not to call him a

lowlife drug addict and a lowdown cheater. "Well, it's not like *you* were ever gonna buy her one. You don't even pay bills the way you're supposed to. You've never done anything except use my sister."

"Alexis, you need to mind your own business," Sabrina said.

"Yeah," Melvin said, quickly agreeing. "You just mind your own little uppity business."

"Say whatever you want, Melvin, but you and I both know that if you were helping my sister, your heat wouldn't be shut off. She also wouldn't have had to ask me to pay your electric bill last week."

Melvin tossed Sabrina a dirty look. "I thought you told me you borrowed that money from one of your friends."

Sabrina ignored him. "Courtney, I said get your things so we can go. Do it now! And didn't I tell you to give your aunt her phone back?"

Courtney gazed at Alexis, reluctantly passed her the phone and then went into the guest bedroom.

"Sabrina, did you hear me?" Melvin asked.

"Yeah, I heard you, but my friend didn't have it."

"So you went ahead and asked this thing right here, even though I've told you I don't want her handouts."

Alexis wondered if she was daydreaming. Melvin didn't pay any bills, but he was dictating who Sabrina borrowed money from? This was like watching some outrageous comedy show, except there wasn't a thing funny about it.

Alexis tried to calm herself down and speak a little

softer than she had been. "Look, Sabrina, why don't you just let Courtney stay here for a few days. At least until you get your heat back on."

"Our heat *is* back on. Or at least it will be by this evening."

"Really? How?"

"How do you think, Miss Know-It-All?" Melvin chimed in. "With money."

"Surely not with yours. And to tell you the truth, I don't believe a word you're saying. Not either of you."

"Believe what you want!" Sabrina spat. "I don't have to prove anything to you."

"Well, you kinda do. Because if that heat isn't on, and you take Courtney out of here, I'm calling the authorities."

Melvin laughed. "This trick right here is somethin' else, and that's why I told you not to ask her for anything."

Alexis lowered her eyebrows. "You know what? I want you outta here, Melvin. Get out of my house, and don't ever bring your worthless behind back here."

"I never wanted to come here in the first place. The only reason I'm here is to get my daughter. Now, for the last time, Courtney, you get your stuff together and get out here!"

Alexis stared at Sabrina. "So you're really gonna make Courtney suffer? You're gonna make her sleep in that cold house?"

"Girl, didn't I tell you the bill was paid? Are you deaf?"

"No, but I don't believe you, either. You've lied about bills being paid before."

"Well, I'm not lying now."

Courtney came out of the room with her bag. She carried her coat on her arm, though. Alexis was sure she hadn't put it on because she was hoping that at some point her parents might say she could stay.

"I'm not letting you take her back to that icebox, Sabrina," Alexis said.

"You make me sick, Alexis!" Sabrina opened her large handbag, pulled out a receipt, and jammed it against Alexis's chest. When it fell to the floor, Alexis picked it up. Surprisingly, it really was a receipt stamped with today's date.

"Satisfied?" Sabrina said. "Is that enough proof for you, Judge Judy?"

"I really wish you would let her stay with me for a while," Alexis said, trying her best to sound as cordial as possible. "I'll take good care of her, and it will also give you guys a chance to get on your feet."

"We don't need any help from you," Melvin said, walking down the hallway to the front door and opening it. "Let's go, Sabrina and Courtney."

"Aunt Lexi?" Courtney said with pleading eyes.

Alexis hugged her. "I'll call you later, and you'll be fine."

"On whose phone?" Sabrina asked. " She just gave you back the phone you bought for her, and you certainly won't be calling her on mine. Courtney is *my* daughter, and I want you to stay away from her."

Sabrina grabbed Courtney by the arm and snatched her toward the hallway. Courtney burst into tears, and when the door closed, Alexis did the same. She'd told herself she wouldn't cry about anything today, but now here she was. Her poor niece was living an awful life, and there wasn't a thing she could do about it. Alexis could make a complaint to CPS the way she'd threatened, but she just didn't feel right about turning in her sister. If she did, their relationship would be over for good.

Alexis sat back down on the sofa, totally beside herself. It just seemed that if there wasn't one thing there was another. She felt as though she'd lost everyone, and as she scanned the photos on her fireplace mantel, her spirit dropped to an all-time low. First, she stared at the one of her, Sabrina, and their parents when she and Sabrina were only one and three years old. Then she looked at her parents' wedding photo, but soon moved on to a photo of just her and her mom, the one that had been taken about a year before her mom had passed. After that, she gazed at three different photos of Courtney: one from when she was a newborn, one when she was in kindergarten, and one from the birthday party Alexis had given for her back in May. She looked so happy.

Alexis scanned the photos back and forth, but then she glanced at the photo of her and Chase on the far end. She'd accompanied him to one of Borg-Freeman's executive dinners, and they'd hired a photographer for it. Chase was so handsome and very kind, and she remembered how she'd felt like Cinderella at the ball.

But that was the past.

So she got up, turned out the light in the family room, grabbed a bottle of water from the kitchen, and went to her bedroom. Normally, she debated whether she needed to take a sleeping pill, but not tonight. It was barely after five, yet she opened the bottle and swallowed two of them as quickly as she could. She didn't care how early it was. All she knew was that she didn't want to feel any more pain. She didn't want to think about the fact that she was alone and unhappy or that her feelings of depression were getting worse. So much so that it was starting to scare her. She didn't want to die, but she'd be lying if she said she hadn't thought about how pain-free she would be. What was strange was that even though she had these kinds of thoughts, she was sure no one around her had ever suspected it. Maybe the reason they hadn't was because Alexis only allowed them to see what they were used to: the strong, determined, and highly independent woman they'd always known her to be. Of course, she'd shared with Paula and Chase that the holidays were very hard for her, but mostly what she did was smile and laugh the way everyone expected her to. For the most part, she appeared to be happy, and she saved her moments of deep sadness for when she was locked away at home. Like now.

Soon, though, she'd be fast asleep, and she wouldn't feel a thing. At least not until tomorrow.

Chapter 14

Alexis forced her eyes open, but in all honesty, she dreaded facing another day. She wasn't in the mood, but she sat up anyway to check her phones. She only did it, though, in case Courtney had tried to contact her. Alexis wasn't sure how Courtney would be able to, since she no longer had her cell phone, but there was a chance she might use someone else's if she needed Alexis. However, after checking the caller ID screens on both her home phone and her smartphone, she saw nothing. Not a single person had called her. Finally, she checked her email and saw that Tracey needed answers to a few questions, and that she'd also sent information on two new speaking engagement requests. Tracey was truly amazing and had been such a godsend for seven years. She had a full-time job working as a marketing specialist, but she still worked part-time for Alexis. She was also a great friend, someone with a truly kind heart, and Alexis wasn't sure what she would do without her.

Alexis sat on the side of her bed, thinking about the day before, and it wasn't long before she thought about Chase and their breakup. It almost didn't seem real, but Alexis knew it was *very* real, because she had been the one to end it. He hadn't dropped by to get his ring, but if he didn't come pick it up by early next week, she would take it to his office and leave it with his executive assistant. He also had several pieces of clothing in her closet, but instead of taking those to his place of business, she would mail them to his home. It was funny how quickly and drastically life could change. One minute she'd been happily engaged to one of the most eligible bachelors in town, and the next, she'd become miserably single. It was just the way things tended to work out for her these days, so she shouldn't have been surprised.

Then, adding insult to injury, Alexis thought about Courtney and her run-in with Sabrina and Melvin again. She knew they were Courtney's parents, and that she didn't have a lot of say-so in the way they were raising Courtney, but she couldn't help worrying about the kind of life they were subjecting her to. It was so unfair to Courtney, and she hadn't asked to be treated this way. She also hadn't asked for a mother who basically had done nothing except party from the time her daughter had been born. Sabrina would leave Courtney with their mom to babysit, and there were times when she hadn't come back for days. She would leave and act as though she didn't have a child, and that had always annoyed Alexis. Their mother hadn't done much complaining, but Alexis had felt that Sabrina should have spent a lot more time with Courtney. She'd also thought that if Sabrina didn't want to take care of her own daughter, she could have at least given their mom a break sometimes and allowed Alexis to keep her. But Sabrina had rarely allowed her to because of how strained their own relationship had been. Thankfully, Courtney and Alexis had still become very close, since Alexis had spent lots of time with her at their mom's house. Sadly, though, now that their mom was gone, Alexis only got to spend quality time with her niece every now and then. After yesterday, her visits with Courtney were likely to lessen even more.

So there it was. No future husband, no mother, and no niece.

Alexis walked through her house, looked out the window, and saw that it was snowing. She'd heard yesterday during the weather report that there was a chance of it, but she hadn't thought they'd get much of anything. It was coming down pretty good, too, and although the snow was beautiful, Alexis was glad she didn't have to be out in it.

She peered out the window until her phone rang. She didn't want to talk to anyone, but when she went back into her bedroom and saw that it was Paula, she answered the call.

"Hey," she said.

"How are you?"

"Don't even ask."

"Uh-oh. What has Mommy Dearest done now?" Paula asked, laughing.

"To make a long story short, she faked a few stroke symptoms, called Renee to the hospital, and Chase and I broke up."

"Broke up?"

Alexis could almost see the frustrated look on Paula's face.

"Yep, it's over."

"Who broke up with who?"

"I broke up with him."

"Because of his mother?"

"Yep. She was never gonna stop, and I just couldn't deal with that."

"I really wish you would have hung in there, because Chase really loves you, Lex."

"I love him, too, and I miss him, but I also believe I made the right decision."

"So this happened yesterday?"

"Yeah. Yesterday morning."

"Why didn't you call me?"

"I didn't wanna bother you with that, plus I ended up going to pick up Courtney. That's a whole other story, but I'll tell you about that another time."

"You wanna meet for lunch?"

"Can I take a rain check? I really don't feel like going out today."

"I don't blame you. It's snowing, and I hear it's getting pretty slick out there. I'll just call you later."

"Sounds good, and you be careful on your way home."

"I will. Love you, girl."

"Love you, too."

Alexis went into her office and sat in front of her computer. She wasn't planning to take off her pajamas, but she decided that maybe she should try to get some work done. For one, she still needed to answer all of Tracey's emails, and she also needed to work more on her speech for the university. But the longer she sat there, not opening her emails or doing anything work-related, the farther her mind drifted into depressing territory. She wondered why she couldn't make herself feel better. Why she'd turned into someone she barely knew. Why she cried all the time, the same as she was doing now.

Fortunately, she knew how to make it all go away. It was only nine thirty in the morning, but she took two more sleeping pills and did her usual: got back in bed, closed her eyes, and curled into a ball. If she had things her way, she'd sleep until tomorrow. Or better yet, a lot longer.

Chapter 15

*I*nstead of sleeping only through yesterday, Alexis had slept just about nonstop, forty-eight hours straight. She'd awakened on Friday evening for all of ten minutes, but that was only because Paula had called to check on her and her pills had started to wear off. She'd felt groggy enough to fall back to sleep, however, once she'd assured Paula that she was okay and just wanted to rest, she'd gotten up and gone to the bathroom. After that, she'd continued on to the kitchen, thinking she might get something to eat, but when she realized she still didn't have an appetite, she'd pulled a bottle of water from the refrigerator and moseyed right back into her bedroom. Unsurprisingly, she'd taken two more sleeping pills, making sure she slept through the night. Then, yesterday, she'd slept on and off throughout the day and hadn't answered any calls, not even those from Paula and two of her aunts, because she'd just wanted to sleep.

Now, here it was Sunday morning, and she didn't feel much different. This was also the reason she frowned and

sighed all at the same time when she heard her doorbell. She had no idea who was showing up unannounced,
and she had a mind to ignore them. But whoever it was
wouldn't go away. They just kept ringing the bell, over
and over, the way some children do.

Alexis slipped on her robe in a huff and went to the door.
At first, she was sort of shocked to see that it was Paula, but
then she remembered turning off the ringer on both her
phones so she wouldn't be disturbed. There was no doubt that
Paula had called more than once and was now worried sick.

Alexis opened the door.

Paula wasted no time going in on her. "Why haven't
you been answering your phone? I called you three times
last night, and then when you didn't answer this morning
I knew it was time to come by here."

Paula walked in like she owned the place, removed her
coat, tossed it on a chair, and sat down. Alexis still hadn't
said a word, and although Paula was her best friend,
Alexis hoped she wasn't planning to stay very long. She
looked to be dressed for church, though, so chances were
she'd be leaving pretty quickly.

"And you look a mess," she declared. "Lex, what's going on? And why do you look so exhausted?"

"I'm fine," she said, sitting down across from Paula.

"Look, girl, this is me you're talking to. I know fine
when I see it, and you look nothing like that. I think
you're depressed about Chase."

"I just need some time alone is all. I have a lot on my
mind, but I'll get through this."

Paula folded her arms. "I know you think you made the right decision, Lex, but you never should have broken up with that man. Not when he loves you as much as he does, and especially not because of his mother."

"You don't understand. Geneva was never going to give up. She was always going to be a problem. She might not have been able to stop Chase from marrying me, but can you imagine all the heartache she would have caused me once I became her daughter-in-law? I told you...I've heard too many horror stories from other women, and to me it's just not worth it."

"But eventually, I think Chase would have put a stop to it."

"I don't. Deep down he knows who his mother is, but he doesn't want to hurt her or tell her to move out, either. He loves both of us, and that made him feel as though he was caught in the middle."

"Still," Paula said, "I think you should have tried to work things out with him."

"Well, he knows why I called off our engagement, but it's not like he's burning up my phone line trying to contact me. He hasn't called since it happened."

"I'm sure he will, though, because he really does love you. I don't think I've ever seen a man look at a woman the way he looks at you, and I've certainly never known you to be in love with any man the way you love Chase. The two of you are meant to be together. Period."

Alexis stroked her hair back with both hands and wondered how long they were going to have to talk about this.

"And what were you going to tell me about Courtney?" Paula asked.

"She called me because their heat was shut off, and then she told me that sometimes they don't have food to eat."

"You have got to be kidding! What's wrong with Sabrina?"

"I don't know, but we really had it out on Thursday. I regret getting into it with her, though, because now she's going to make it even harder for me to see Courtney. That no-good Melvin also came over here, acting a complete fool."

"I wish I'd been here. I know it's none of my business, but you know I can't stand him. I'm surprised he even has a job. He's so useless, and doesn't care a thing about your sister or his daughter. Maybe you should report them. Not to get Sabrina into trouble, but so that maybe she'll wake up and make some changes."

"I thought about that, and I even threatened her with it, but I'm hoping she'll eventually just get rid of Melvin."

"Yeah, well, she hasn't gotten rid of him in all these years."

"I know, but I still keep praying for her to change. I won't let Courtney keep going without, though, and if I don't hear from her soon, I'll go to her school to check on her. At least Sabrina has me down as someone who can go there and even pick Courtney up if I need to."

Paula glanced at her watch. "We still have a couple of hours before the second service begins, so why don't you ride to church with me?"

"I'm not up to it."

"I really think you'd feel better if you did. You've been locked up in this house for three days, and it's time you get out of here."

"Not today."

"Pretty please," Paula said, smiling. "I know you don't feel like it, but maybe going to church will make you feel better."

"Nope."

"Well, okay," Paula said, standing. "Can I at least go pick you up some breakfast and bring it back?"

"I'm not hungry."

"When was the last time you ate?"

"I told you I'm fine, so don't worry about me."

"You're my girl, Lex, and I'm concerned. You seem really depressed to me, and I don't like it."

"Tomorrow will be a new day and a new week, and I'll be good. You'll see."

Paula looked at her, clearly not believing a word Alexis was saying, but she didn't argue. "I'll call you this afternoon."

Alexis walked her to the front entryway, and Paula turned and hugged her.

"I love you, Lex, and I'm here for you. Always."

"I know that. And I love you, too."

Alexis closed the door behind her and watched her get into her car and drive away. Then she went back to bed. She was asleep in no time.

Chapter 16

*U*ghhh!" Alexis said, cringing when she heard her cell phone ringing. She'd only decided to turn the ringer back on because she'd still been hoping she might hear from Courtney. She didn't want to take the chance of Courtney calling and then having to leave a message, especially if she needed to talk to Alexis immediately.

Alexis pulled the phone from her nightstand and should have known it was Paula again.

"Hello?" she said, attempting to sound sleepier than she was.

"Girl, you need to get dressed, and I mean dressed in a hurry."

Alexis sat straight up in her bed. "Why?"

"Because Pastor Black and I are on our way over."

"You know what? This joke of yours isn't funny, Paula."

"I'm not joking. I'm leaving the church parking lot right now, and he's gonna follow me."

"Why are you bringing him over here? You know this isn't a good time for me." Alexis couldn't remember ever being so upset with Paula.

"Look, Lex. I know asking Pastor Black to come for a visit might seem a little drastic, but you're depressed. You're not getting better, and I'm not about to sit around watching you get worse. You looked drugged, you sound drugged, and you haven't even combed your hair. So if you're mad at me, I'm fine with that."

"You had no right inviting him over here, Paula. You've really gone too far this time."

"Maybe. But while you're sitting there trying to chastise me, I suggest you spend these next fifteen minutes getting dressed. Because that's all the time you have."

"Paula, please tell Pastor Black that I'm okay, and that he doesn't need to come here."

"You're still wasting time, I see. By now, you could have brushed your teeth and thrown on some clothes."

"Bye, Paula," Alexis said, tossing her phone on the bed. She was so irritated. And who did this kind of thing? Going to the senior pastor of a huge congregation and asking him to casually drop by some member's home. Then, the idea that he'd agreed to come could only mean one thing: Paula had told him everything that was going on with Alexis and Chase. Alexis would deal with her later, though, because now she had no choice but to rush and get ready.

Alexis had barely finished combing her hair and pulling it back into a ponytail when Paula and Pastor

Black arrived. When she opened the door, she saw that Miss Lana, Pastor Black's senior assistant and office manager, had come as well. It was common knowledge that Miss Lana was also Pastor Black's mother figure.

"Please come in," Alexis said.

Miss Lana and Pastor Black hugged Alexis, but Alexis gave Paula an evil eye. She still couldn't believe her friend had gone to such extremes.

"We can have a seat in my family room," Alexis said.

"If it's okay with you," Miss Lana said, "Paula and I will excuse ourselves to another room. That way you and Pastor can speak privately."

"Of course. Paula knows where my den is, if that's okay."

"That'll be fine," Miss Lana said, smiling, and the two of them left the room.

Pastor Black set his black wool coat on the arm of the sofa and unbuttoned his suit jacket. Then he sat in one of the chairs. "So, how are you?"

"I can hang your coat up if you'd like," Alexis offered.

"No, it's fine. But how are you, Alexis?" he asked again.

"Pretty good. And let me just say, too, that it really wasn't necessary for you to drive all the way over here. Especially since nothing's wrong with me. You should be having dinner with your family."

"It's not a problem. Charlotte and the children are over in Chicago visiting her parents for the day, but she wanted me to give you her best. I spoke to her after service."

Alexis smiled. "Please tell her I said thanks."

Not a lot of folks liked their church's first lady, because of some of the terrible things she'd done over the years, but she and Alexis had always gotten along. Maybe it was because Alexis worked pretty closely with her on their women's ministry, and Alexis tried not to judge her. Alexis didn't agree with some of what Sister Black had done in the past, but she didn't focus on that. Instead, she treated Sister Black the way Sister Black treated her, and they had a good relationship. Sister Black's absence, however, did explain why Miss Lana had ridden over with Pastor Black, because he'd long stopped visiting female parishioners alone. Either Sister Black, Miss Lana, or one of the deacons or male elders in the church accompanied him. That way there was no risk of rumors, lies, or other problems that might occur.

Pastor Black rested his elbows on either arm of the chair. "So, I hear you broke off your engagement with Chase."

Alexis wasn't shocked that Paula had told him, but she still shook her head. "Paula really shouldn't have bothered you with this."

"Well, actually, she didn't. All she said was that you were very depressed. Chase is the one who told me about your breakup. He and I had lunch yesterday to talk about it. He'd asked me if I would talk to you, too, and I was planning to call you tomorrow. But when Paula came to my office before service, I decided it was best I talk with you today."

"It just wasn't working out," she said.

"Is that the only thing bothering you?"

Alexis wanted to tell him she was fine, but at this point she was tired of saying that. So she told him everything.

"It's my breakup with Chase, it's the problems I'm having with my sister, and I'm worried about my niece. And then, Pastor, I know it's been five years and maybe I should feel better about the holidays, but I still miss my mom."

"The Christmas holiday season is tough for a lot of people, but you have to find peace with your mom's death. Your mom is gone to a place where people never want to come back from. She wouldn't come back here even if she could. She's with God, she's at rest, and we can rejoice in knowing that."

"I am happy that she's no longer suffering, but the selfish part of me wants her here. Her brain tumor wasn't even malignant, but it still took her life. I know it's wrong, but I can't seem to get beyond that. And I mean, who expects to lose their mother at such a young age? I was only thirty-three when she passed."

"I know you miss her, but maybe you should try to focus on what she told you right before she made her transition. Remember when she said she wanted you to pick up where she left off? She said she wanted you to go on to do all the things she'd prayed that you would do, and she wanted you to be happy."

Alexis cried silent tears, periodically wiping them away. "I'm such a strong person, and I'm such a believer in God's Word, but for some reason I feel like I'm falling apart."

"Well, for one thing, you need to give Chase another chance. He told me about the problems you were having with his mother, and although I know firsthand how Sister Dupont can be sometimes, that's still Chase's mother, and it's not always easy for any son to see his mother as a troublemaker. I'm not here to judge her or take sides with either of you, but no matter what, I believe you and Chase were made for each other."

"But Pastor, his mother lied on me, and he believed her."

"No, I think it's more that he *wanted* to believe her."

"Maybe. And then there's the way she talks to me and treats me. Well, I just can't live like that."

"I understand, and that's the reason I told Chase that he's going to have to be a man about this. He's going to have to set some boundaries for his mother and hold her to them."

"She'll never go for that. Geneva thinks that just because she's rich, she can say or do whatever she wants."

"But if she wants to have a relationship with her son, she'll change her attitude. The Bible says, 'Therefore shall a man leave his father and his mother, and shall cleave unto his wife, and they shall be one flesh,' so Sister Dupont is going to have to accept that."

Alexis didn't comment, because she respectfully disagreed with Pastor Black. She knew the scripture was correct, and she wholeheartedly believed it, but Geneva Dupont wasn't changing anything for anybody.

Pastor Black went on. "Well, are you at least willing to talk to Chase?"

"I don't know. I still love him, but I don't wanna be hurt again."

"I really think you should hear him out. And if you're okay with it, I'll tell him to call you this afternoon."

Part of Alexis desperately wanted to hear Chase's voice, but part of her wanted to leave things as they were. She didn't know what to do, and thankfully, Pastor Black changed the subject a bit. He asked about her strained relationship with her sister, and said he'd be praying for both of them.

Finally, when Pastor Black, Paula, and Miss Lana had left, Alexis sat back down on her sofa. She still hadn't told Pastor Black it was okay to have Chase call her, but now she sort of wished she had. She even wished she had the courage to do the calling herself—or the will to recite the Christmas prayer she'd written. But she didn't. So, instead, she curled up on her sofa and did nothing—except wallow in more sadness.

Chapter 17

Alexis stroked another coat of mascara across her eye-
lashes, brushed some pressed powder across her face, and
added some lip gloss. It had been five days since she'd
flat-ironed and curled her hair in a presentable style, gotten completely dressed in a nice sweater and a pair of
jeans, and put on some makeup. Last night, she'd still felt
a bit depressed, but this morning was a new day and she
had to admit her change in attitude and upbeat spirit had
a lot to do with her mother. Yesterday, Pastor Black had
reminded Alexis about her mother's words, and for some
reason she hadn't been able to stop thinking about them.
She'd replayed those words over and over in her mind last
night and then again early this morning. That was also
the reason she hadn't taken any sleeping pills, and she
wasn't planning to take them again. She could even hear
her mother's words in her head right now: "Alexis, I want
you to pick up where I left off. I want you to go on to do

all the things I prayed that you would do, but more than anything, I want you to be happy."

So, this morning, while lying in bed, Alexis had made up her mind to fight her way out of her depression any way she could. Then, shortly after getting up, she'd heard from Chase. She hadn't expected it, but he'd called her two hours ago, saying he was taking the day off and wanted to know if he could come by to see her. She'd been sort of surprised, since this was the week his company was launching its new product, but she hadn't questioned him. She'd also wondered if Pastor Black had told him to call her, even though she'd never agreed to it, but she didn't inquire about that, either. She was just glad he was on his way to her house, and that he would be there shortly.

Alexis picked up a copy of the Christmas prayer she'd written. She'd read it multiple times this morning, and now she read it again. She particularly focused on the part that said *I pray that You will bless others who are hurting as well, and that You will eliminate all sadness and loneliness completely.* She was tired of feeling sad and tired of taking pills, and she also didn't want to be alone anymore.

Alexis gave herself a once-over in her large vanity mirror and heard her bell ringing. She wasn't sure why, but she felt as though she were meeting Chase for the first time. She even felt a bit nervous and tried to calm herself. As she stood at her door, she inhaled and exhaled and then opened it. Chase looked as wonderful as ever. He had on a black wool turtleneck sweater, black dress pants, and a short black cashmere coat. And he smelled so good. She'd recognize Extreme by Tom Ford anywhere, as it was Chase's favorite cologne. Alexis must have been a fool to break up with this man.

"Hey," she said, smiling.

Chase walked inside. "Hey, beautiful. How are you?"

"I'm well," she said, closing the door and walking through the hallway. But before she could take another step, Chase pulled her by her arm, gently pushed her against the wall, and kissed her. Alexis didn't bother trying to resist him, because she'd only be pretending if she did. Their kiss was passionate and intense, and Alexis prayed he wouldn't ask to make love to her, because she feared she might be too weak to say no this time. She was so emotionally bankrupt and terribly confused about a number of things, and she didn't trust what she might go along with. Especially since she really wanted him. It had always been a struggle, remaining celibate, because she already knew how fabulous Chase made her feel. But today, the struggle was much more challenging.

Thankfully, Chase pulled away slightly and simply hugged her. He held her tight, seemingly not wanting to let her go.

"I love you, Lexi. You're everything to me, and my life just doesn't work without you."

They held each other close, speaking no words.

"We have to work this out," he said.

"I want that, too," she said, "but..."

"Let's sit down," he told her.

They went and sat on the sofa.

Chase turned his body slightly toward her. "Pastor Black told me he came by here yesterday."

"Is that why you called me?" Before he'd arrived, she'd decided not to ask him, but for some reason she wanted to know.

"No, as a matter of fact, he told me he didn't think you were ready and that I might need to give you more time. But I couldn't wait for that. I wanted to see you now. It's the reason I took off work, even though this is one of the worst weeks for me to do something like that. But working things out with you is a lot more important."

"You didn't have to do that. I know this is a crucial time for the company."

"It'll be fine. I also want you to know that I spoke to Margaret."

"Oh, really?"

"I did, and she confirmed that it hadn't been until you called my mother to say you were coming over that she asked her to drop off some clothing at the cleaners. What got me, though, was that she volunteered some other information I hadn't asked for."

"What?"

"She told me that the clothes Mother gave her had just come from the cleaners the week before, and she hadn't worn them yet. She said when she got back that afternoon, she was in Mother's bathroom and saw the cleaner tags in her wastebasket."

Alexis shook her head in amazement. "Goodness."

"And that's not all. Mother also told her to then stop by the grocery store to pick up some of the same items she'd asked her to buy on Friday. She made up errands for Margaret to run so she wouldn't hear what really went on with your visit. So you were right about everything. I'm really sorry I didn't want to believe you. My mother has done a lot of things that I wasn't happy about, but lying on you the way she did, that was the worst."

"She just doesn't like me, and I doubt she ever will."

"Well, whether she does or doesn't, I'm not giving you up. I also thought about the whole Renee thing, and I don't blame you for being upset about her. Mother was wrong for suddenly befriending her, and Renee was wrong for hanging around the way she did. She knew what Mother was up to, and I could tell she was enjoying it."

"Hmmph," Alexis said. "She not only enjoyed it, she's still hoping she has a chance with you."

"If she does, she's wasting her time, because I'm not interested."

"So now what?"

"I need you to trust that I'm going to make things right."

"But how?"

"I'm going to have that talk with my mother. The only difference now is that you're going to be with me when I do."

Alexis wasn't sure if she liked that idea or not. It was one thing for Chase to sit down with his mother on his own, but including her might only make Geneva despise her more. She would see Alexis as the enemy who had turned her son against her, and she would hate her for it. Geneva hated her now, but after this "talk," her hatred would rise to an infinite level.

"I'm not sure that's the right thing to do," she said.

"If I'm going to make Mother understand how much I love you, and that it's time she accept you as her future daughter-in-law, it's the only way."

"When are you planning to do this?"

"In a couple of hours."

"I don't know, Chase."

"I want you there so that my mother fully understands what I expect from her. She needs to know what I won't tolerate any longer."

"Okay, if that's what you feel we need to do."

"It is. Although it might help if you put your ring back on," he said, smiling.

Alexis smiled, too, and went into her bedroom. When she returned with the ring in her hand, Chase took it from her.

"There's no turning back this time, so you need to be sure," he said.

"I'm positive. But I want you to know that I'm never going to be the diehard socialite your mother thinks I should be, and I'm never going to think that wearing high-priced clothing is important. I'm always going to be me, and money or marrying you won't change that."

"I would never expect anything different. I fell in love

with you because of who you already are, not because of who I want you to become."

Alexis gazed at him and held out her left ring finger.

Chase slowly slipped the ring on and then leaned over and kissed her.

"For as long as I live, there will never be another woman for me. You've brought a certain kind of meaning to my life, the right kind of substance, and I will always be grateful to you for that."

"You've changed my life for the better also. And I love you from the bottom of my soul."

"I hope you mean that, because there's a quick stop I want us to make before we go talk to my mother."

"Really? Where?"

"It's a surprise."

Alexis had no idea what it could be, but knowing Chase, the surprise would be well worth her while. She was sure she would love it.

Chapter 18

Chase slipped his key in the lock of his front door, and Alexis stepped into the entryway. She wasn't looking forward to this meeting with Geneva—a meeting Geneva didn't know Alexis was attending—and she could just about imagine how horribly this was all going to turn out. Chase was clearly hoping for the best and expecting his mother to be reasonable, but Alexis secretly remained pessimistic. Mothers like Geneva didn't change just because someone wanted them to. Instead, they dug their heels in for all eternity. They stood their ground, made harsh demands, and expected anyone who disagreed with them to surrender. It was simply the nature of the beast, and today would be no different.

"How are you, Miss Fletcher?" Margaret said, taking her long wool coat.

"I'm fine, but when are you going to start calling me Alexis?"

Margaret moved closer to her and whispered in her ear, "As soon as Mrs. Dupont moves out of here."

Alexis quietly chuckled, because she'd known for months that this was the only reason Margaret was always so formal with her. With Geneva, everything always had to be so prim and proper, but things would be different once Alexis and Chase were married. Alexis would see Margaret as a friend who just so happened to work for them, and she would treat her like family.

As they walked toward the living room, Chase looked up the winding staircase. "Mother, can you come down here?"

It took a few seconds, but then Alexis heard her say, "Coming, son. I'll be right down."

Chase and Alexis sat next to each other, and Geneva finally walked in. As usual, she was all decked out in fancy attire.

"Oh, I didn't realize you were bringing someone with you."

"Not someone, Mother. Alexis."

Alexis knew Chase meant business because he wasn't even using his pet name for her. At the moment, she was Alexis all the way.

Geneva sat in the same chair she'd been in the day Alexis had come to visit her. "So, what was it you wanted to talk to me about?"

"You've said and done some things to Alexis that I'm not happy about, and I want you to apologize to her."

"You can't be serious?"

"I'm dead serious. I'm in love with Alexis, she's going to be my wife, and I need her to feel comfortable around you."

"So let me get this straight. You want me, your own mother, to apologize to the woman who attacked me? The woman who threatened me and destroyed a three-thousand-dollar vase?"

Three thousand dollars? Just *hearing* the price made Alexis want to gasp.

But Chase didn't seem bothered in the least. "Alexis would never do something like that. She would never do any of the things you told me she did."

Geneva's eyes turned cold. "She would, and she did, Chase. This woman you claim to be so in love with is evil, and she'll never be a good wife to you. If you marry her, you'll be making the biggest mistake of your life."

"I'll take my chances," he said, still not moved by her insults.

"Can't you see what a bad influence this woman is? Just look at you! Running around here acting like some naïve schoolboy. I mean, what corporate CEO takes the day off to spend it with his girlfriend? It's simply ludicrous."

"Mother, you'll never understand what Alexis and I have, because you and Dad had something very different."

Geneva frowned. "Don't you dare bring your father into this."

"I'm just saying, Mother. You and Dad were married for a very long time, but you never had the kind of loving relationship a husband and wife should have."

Geneva seemed frustrated and embarrassed. "So now you think you can talk to me any way you want? You never did that until she came into the picture. You should be ashamed of yourself, Chase."

"I'm sorry, Mother, but I need you to accept Alexis as your daughter-in-law."

"I can't do that. Not when she's going to ruin your entire reputation. The woman was raised on the west side of Mitchell, for God's sake. How can *anyone* accept her? Certainly not me, and definitely none of your colleagues."

"Okay, Mother, you know what? Here's the deal: Alexis and I are getting married, and that's that. It's also time you move back to your own home."

Geneva covered her mouth. "Oh my God. You've really let this woman turn you against me. You're actually kicking your own mother out on the street?"

"I'm doing no such thing. You're my mother, I love you, and you'll always be welcome here. Nothing will ever change that."

"Fine, I'll move out after the holidays."

"No, I'm having someone from our shipping department bring over a few boxes. That way Margaret can start packing your things for you, and you'll be able to move back home by the end of next week."

Geneva stood up, flaring her hands. "Chase, please just stop it. What difference does it make if I wait until after the holidays? You're not even getting married until June."

"Well, actually, there's been a change of plans. We're now getting married on Christmas Eve."

From the look on Geneva's face, Alexis wondered if she was going to pass out. This was the surprise Chase had told Alexis about. They'd left her house and driven to the courthouse. Alexis hadn't realized why they were there until he'd turned off his engine and said, "Let's not wait until June. Let's get married this month. Unless you really want a huge ceremony." Alexis had smiled, hugged him, and told him she didn't need all that. All she wanted was for them to become husband and wife and be happy.

Geneva still seemed flustered, but Chase kept talking. "We just finished, applying for our marriage license. So this is a done deal, Mother."

"Well, if nothing else, I sure hope Jerry can get your prenup handled that quickly."

Chase lowered his eyebrows. "Prenup? No, Mother, I guess you still don't understand. There won't be one. I love Alexis, and once we get married, everything I have will become hers. I'm also adding her name to the title of this house."

"You've lost your ever-loving mind!" she shouted as if she were crazy.

"No, I'm doing things the right way, and I really want your blessing."

"Well, you can just forget that, because I'll never be okay with this joke of a marriage."

Chase stood up. "Fine, Mother. Suit yourself," he said, and then reached for Alexis's hand. "Baby, let's go. I told Pastor Black we'd be there by two o'clock."

"What are you seeing Pastor Black for?" Geneva asked.

"Since we're moving up our date, we need to have our final counseling session."

Geneva shook her head in disgust but didn't say anything else until they turned to walk out of the room.

"You're really breaking my heart, son. That woman just isn't good enough for you. Do you think your father's parents would have allowed him to marry *me*, had I not come from the right kind of family? Do you really think this woman could ever be a true Dupont? She'll never fit in, and all she's going to do is bring down our name. She'll ruin everything we've worked for."

Chase stared at his mother.

He and Alexis walked out and never looked back at her.

Chapter 19

Alexis could tell Chase was hurt and upset about the confrontation he'd just had with his mother. Alexis hadn't been surprised in the least by her comments and responses, but she could tell Chase had truly believed that he would somehow convince Geneva to see things his way. He wanted peace within his family, and he also wanted the two most important women in his life to share some sort of bond. But that just wasn't possible, not with Geneva making it very clear that she would never accept Alexis as her daughter-in-law or give them her blessing. Alexis didn't want a strained relationship with the mother of the man she loved and was getting ready to marry, but she couldn't control Geneva's opinions or ill feelings toward her.

They walked into Pastor Black's executive offices, and Miss Lana smiled and stood up.

She walked around her desk and hugged them. "Well, hello, you two."

"How are you, Miss Lana?" Alexis said.

"Doing great."

"Glad to hear it," Chase told her, smiling.

"Pastor is all ready, so you can go right on in."

"Thank you," they both said.

Chase knocked on Pastor Black's door.

"Come in," he said, and Chase and Alexis entered his office.

"Hey, Alexis," Charlotte said, hugging her. "Hey, Chase."

"How are you, Sister Black?" he said.

"Couldn't be better, and it looks like the two of you are doing pretty well yourselves. My husband here was just telling me that you've worked everything out, and that you're now getting married on Christmas Eve. I'm so excited and happy for you both."

"So am I," Pastor Black said. "Not to mention, I'm a pretty good matchmaker, if I must say so myself."

They all laughed.

Chase pulled Alexis toward him by her waist. "I'm laughing, but in all honesty, Pastor, you couldn't have done better if you tried. This is the woman I've been waiting for all my life, and I'll always be grateful to you for that."

"No thanks needed. I saw two amazing people with huge hearts, and I thought you should get to know each other."

"Well, I really have to run," Charlotte said, "but Alexis, why don't we plan on having lunch after the holidays? Of course, I'll definitely be here for your ceremony as well."

"Sounds good."

Charlotte said her good-byes, and Pastor Black, Alexis, and Chase sat down.

Pastor Black leaned his elbows onto his desk and crossed his arms. "So, Chase, how did the visit with your mother go?"

Chase shook his head and relaxed farther into his chair. "It was a disaster. She was worse than ever, and she said so many awful things to Alexis that I didn't even recognize her."

"I was so hoping that talking to her together might help, but it sounds like she's not going to budge on this."

"She just doesn't like me," Alexis said. "And when a woman doesn't like another woman..."

"Well," Pastor Black said, "let's hope she won't feel this way forever."

"I don't know, Pastor," Chase said. "I was a lot more optimistic before today, but now I have to agree with my Lexi here. I'm not sure she'll ever be okay with this."

"As you know, I counsel with a lot of married couples, and sadly, the whole mother-in-law-not-liking-the-future-daughter-in-law thing tends to come up a lot more often than I would like. There are plenty of mothers-in-law who love their daughters-in-law like biological children, but there are also those who just can't stand the idea of another woman being with their son."

"It doesn't make sense to me, though," Chase said.

"Especially when it comes to Alexis, because she's always tried to be nice to Mother. She's also good for me, and she makes me happy, and I would think my mother would be thrilled about that."

"Yeah, you would think so, but unfortunately, it doesn't always turn out like that. Still, I'm going to pray for Sister Dupont's heart."

Alexis would never say it out loud, but it seemed to her that Geneva didn't even have one. She certainly didn't have any compassion or empathy for anyone, and she only cared about her money, worldly possessions, and status. She also didn't have very many friends, except for a few women she called from time to time to boast about some hoity-toity item she'd just purchased or some country club event she'd been asked to chair. Other than that, she didn't seem to have much use for other human beings. She was a cold woman with very little emotion, and to some degree, Alexis felt sorry for her.

"I know this must be very tough for you, Chase," Pastor Black said, "but you can still love and honor your mother and also love the woman you're going to marry. No one, not even family members, should try to dictate who their loved ones end up with, and my advice to you is to move forward as planned. Your mother might not like it, but she's going to have to live with your decision to be with Alexis."

"I just wish she could see how much I love Chase," Alexis said. "I wish she knew that even though Chase loves me, it won't change the way he feels about her."

Pastor Black smiled. "Maybe someday she will. But if not, the two of you have to go on with your lives. I think you should still invite her to the ceremony, and you should also invite her to holiday dinners and anything else you're doing that's family-related. She might not join you, but at least you will have done the right thing."

"I won't stop trying," Chase said, "but after today I can't help but see her in a different light. I've always known she had a standoffish personality and sometimes looked down on certain people, but I never knew she was this bad."

Pastor Black slightly chuckled. "Well, that's because until now you've never asked someone to marry you. She feels like Alexis is taking something from her, and she can't see beyond that. No matter how illogical it is, she believes Alexis is the enemy."

Alexis grabbed Chase's hand. "I'm really sorry about this. I never meant to cause problems between you and your mother."

"Baby, it's not your fault. It's nobody's fault, and I'm just going to pray to move on."

"Well, on a lighter note," Pastor Black said, changing the subject, "are you planning to invite a lot of people to your ceremony or only a few?"

"We've decided to keep it very small," Chase said. "For me it'll be my best friend from childhood and his wife, two of my VPs and their wives, and my executive assistant and her husband. My father's family lives too far away, and of course, my mother doesn't have any family. She was an only child just like me."

"What about you, Alexis?"

"Two of my aunts and their husbands will be there; my best friend, Paula, and her boyfriend; my assistant and her husband; and I'm hoping my sister and my niece will come."

"Sounds good, and along with Charlotte and me, I'm sure Miss Lana will want to attend, if that's okay. She's so happy for both of you."

"Absolutely," Chase said. "We would love to have her."

"We'll be honored," Alexis added.

"And although I don't want to keep bringing your mother up, Chase, you are going to invite her, right?"

"Yeah, I guess. I do want her there, but I also don't want her to try to stop the wedding or turn the entire day into a nightmare."

"We'll all just be prayerful about it. We'll let go and let God. Then, unless the two of you have questions, I do want to leave you with a few pieces of advice. In our first two sessions, we talked about the sanctity of marriage, what marriage means, and how you should keep God at the center of your marriage at all times. But there are also five practical lessons to live by. One, never allow others inside your circle. That means family members, friends, and acquaintances. Keep any problems or disagreements to yourselves and work them out as a couple. Two, never, ever stop dating. Always continue to work at keeping your marriage fun and fresh. Don't ever stop joking around and making each other laugh. Most of all, don't ever stop going places together and hanging out as best friends. Three, don't ever stop communicating. You should never take each other for granted, never go to bed angry, and never stop growing together as a couple. Four, don't ever forget that marriage is what you make it. Marriage requires a lot of hard work, a lot of give-and-take, and lots of understanding and forgiveness. And five, don't ever forget why you fell in love in the first place. Always remember that love bears all things, believes all things, hopes all things, and endures all things. Remember that love never fails," Pastor Black said.

Alexis locked her fingers inside Chase's and thanked God for giving her a man who was full of so much unconditional love, kindness, and integrity. For weeks she'd been feeling depressed, but now she had every reason to hold her head up and be happy. She had a reason to be grateful and to simply live the incredible life she'd been blessed with.

Everything seemed almost perfect—actually, a little too perfect, because no matter how much Alexis wanted to believe that all was well and that nothing would destroy her and Chase's wedding plans, she couldn't get Geneva out of her mind. Chase had explained to his mother that he loved Alexis and that he was marrying her this month, but Alexis wasn't naïve. Women like Geneva just didn't give up that easily, and Alexis wondered when a bomb was going to drop. She had a feeling it might be any day now—or any second.

Chapter 20

_A_s Chase drove his Mercedes S550 away from the church, Alexis read the text message she'd just received from her sister's phone. She was shocked to be hearing from Sabrina.

Aunt Lexi it's an emergency. I just got home. Pls come get us.

Alexis sighed loudly. "Now what?"

Chase looked over at her but quickly focused back on driving. "Honey, what is it?"

"I thought my sister was texting me, but it's from Courtney. She says she needs me to come get them, and that it's an emergency."

"Where do they live?"

"Not far. Just two blocks down this way," she said pointing. "And then to your right."

Thank God they'd just been leaving the church and that Sabrina and Courtney lived near there. Alexis was worried sick, because there was no telling what was going on. She couldn't stop thinking about Courtney and hoped she was okay. She also wondered why Courtney had said to come get "them" and not just her, so she hoped Melvin hadn't done anything stupid. For all Alexis knew he was drugged up and threatening their lives.

Chase turned down the street, and as soon as Alexis spotted her sister's house, her heart sank. Men were carrying out one piece of furniture after another, along with several large boxes. First it had been the electricity that needed to be paid, then the gas had been shut off, and now they were being evicted?

Chase parked across from Sabrina's house, and he and Alexis got out. Sabrina and Melvin stood in the middle of the front lawn, screaming at each other like enemies. Alexis knew Chase didn't act high and mighty like his mother, but she also knew he wasn't used to this kind of drama, and she was so embarrassed.

"How did you let this happen?" Melvin shouted. "This is all your fault!"

"Maybe if you stopped changing jobs, it *wouldn't* be happening!" Sabrina shot back.

Melvin frowned and flipped his hand at her. "Just shut up, Sabrina."

"No, you shut up!"

Alexis saw Courtney rushing toward her. Courtney reached her arms out, lay her head on her aunt's chest, and sobbed. It must have been twenty degrees outside, so she was also shivering. Thankfully, she at least had on a scarf and gloves, and so did Chase and Alexis.

"I'm so sorry, honey," Alexis told her.

"What are we gonna do now, Aunt Lexi? Where are we gonna live?"

"We'll figure something out. So don't you worry about that."

Chase rubbed Courtney's back. "Your aunt is right, sweetheart. Don't you worry about a thing."

Melvin looked over at them with bloodshot eyes. "And what are you doin' here? Both you and your big-time CEO. He's probably never even been on this side of town before."

Alexis took a step forward, but Chase pulled her back.

"Just let him talk, baby. It's not even worth it."

"You better listen to ya boy," he told Alexis. "Comin' over here actin' all tough. Like you really gon' do somethin'. Sabrina, you better check your sister before she get hurt."

All this time, Sabrina hadn't looked at Alexis, and she didn't look now. She was humiliated, and of course, she didn't want to hear anything Alexis had to say.

"Can we come live with you, Aunt Lexi?" Courtney whispered. "I'll beg my dad not to be any trouble. He and my mom can sleep in your other bedroom, and I can sleep on the sofa in your den."

Alexis felt sorry for her niece, and although she and her mother were welcome to stay with her anytime, Melvin would never be allowed there again.

"I'll have to see what your mom wants to do" was all she said.

"Man, that's my stereo you're tossin' around like that!"

Melvin yelled at one of the stockier men. "I oughta knock you dead in your face."

Sabrina grabbed Melvin's arm. "Why don't you just leave them alone before you get into trouble. They're just doin' their jobs."

Melvin yanked away from her and stuck his finger in her face. "Don't you ever put your hands on me."

Alexis loosened Courtney's arms from around her and moved closer to her sister. "Sabrina, come here."

"What?"

"Come here, now!"

Sabrina rolled her eyes but finally walked over. "What is it, Alexis? And please don't ask me what's wrong or how this happened, because I'm not in the mood for that."

"Well, I already know how it happened, but what I don't know is where you're planning to stay tonight."

"I don't know, but we'll be fine."

"That's not good enough. I need to know that you have somewhere to go. Especially Courtney."

"Didn't you hear me when I said we'd be fine? And who asked you to come by here, anyway?"

"What matters is that I'm here. You need help, Sabrina, so why don't you and Courtney just stay with me tonight?"

"And what about Melvin? What do you expect me to do about him? Leave him to fend for himself?"

"I think you and I both know that Melvin isn't invited. My concern is only about you and my niece."

"Why don't you go home, Alexis? Just leave us alone," she said, walking back across the lawn and over toward Melvin. As soon as he saw her approaching him, though, he walked away and kept talking on his cell phone. Sabrina followed him.

"Who are you talkin' to, Melvin?"

Melvin ignored her and walked out into the street.

"I know one thing, it better not be that skank-trick."

Melvin walked back onto the grass, and Sabrina rushed toward him, trying to yank his phone from him.

"Stop it, Sabrina. I'm not playin' with you," he said.

"Give me the phone!" she yelled, still reaching for it.

Melvin held her at arm's length with his other hand and told whoever he was talking to "I'll see you in a few."

"Who was that, Melvin?"

"Don't worry about it. You just figure out where we're gonna live. Because I'm not goin' to no shelter, and I'm definitely not sleepin' in no car."

"The first thing we have to do is find somewhere to store our stuff. We can't just leave it out here like this."

"They can set a match to every piece of this crap for all I care," he said. "It's nothin' but a bunch of cheap junk, anyway. We can get new furniture in a month or so when you file your taxes."

Alexis wanted to slap that idiot. She also wanted to slap some sense into her sister for putting up with this kind of madness. Melvin had never meant her any good, and he was proving it loudly and clearly right now.

Chase wrapped his arm around Courtney and told

Alexis, "Baby, why don't we get back in the car and turn the heat on? Courtney is freezing, and so am I."

"Let's go," she said, but as soon as they turned and started toward the street, Melvin rushed across the yard.

"Where do you think you're takin' my daughter? Courtney, get back over here."

"But Dad, I'm cold."

"Then you go get in your mother's car."

"I asked her if I could when I first got home from school. But she said she didn't want me turning on the car because she doesn't have much gas."

"Well, you're still not gettin' in the car with these snooty buffoons."

Alexis pulled her cell phone from her coat pocket. She was done trying to be nice. "If you don't let this child go warm up in that car, I'm calling CPS right now."

"Call whoever you want."

"No," Sabrina said, walking out to the street. "Go ahead, Courtney."

Chase unlocked the doors, and he and Courtney got inside. Alexis was glad he'd left the car running.

Melvin was hot, though. "Didn't you hear me tell her no?"

"You and I have to start loading up our car," Sabrina said.

Melvin raised his eyebrows. "Did you say *our* car? Because I don't have a car. You let those people pick it up, remember?"

"I didn't *let* them do anything. They picked it up because there was no payment."

"Well, if you'd made the payments like I asked you, I'd still have a way to work and I wouldn't have gotten fired."

Alexis was dumbfounded. The more Sabrina and Melvin argued, the more the plot thickened. So now he didn't have a job or a car? Well then, what *did* he have? And why was Sabrina still hanging on to this hopeless ingrate? Why wouldn't she just dump him and try to make a better life for her and Courtney?

Alexis wasn't sure how this was going to play out, so she decided to go get in the car herself and wait. But just as two of the movers set the living room sofa onto the curb, some woman drove up in an SUV.

Melvin spotted her immediately. "Sabrina, just call me when you find a place. I'm outta here."

Sabrina gazed into the vehicle and recognized the woman. "You're not goin' anywhere with that skank, Melvin. If you leave here, don't ever come back. If you leave, that's it for us."

"Yeah, yeah, yeah," he said, steadily strolling toward his other woman. "That's what you always say."

Sabrina rushed toward him, but he jumped in the SUV, and the woman sped away.

Alexis was speechless. She had no experience with this kind of thing, and her sister's life reminded her of some terrible reality show. Alexis also wondered why Sabrina had chosen to live so differently from the way they'd been raised.

Sabrina turned around, scanning everything sitting on the curb, then gazed over at Alexis. She stared at her for a few seconds and then dropped to her knees in tears. Alexis rushed over and kneeled down next to her. Sabrina wept hysterically.

Chapter 21

It had taken a few hours, but Sabrina and Courtney's personal belongings—and Melvin's, too—were now in storage. Alexis hadn't known exactly how they were going to get it done, but what she did know was that there was no way she was going to let Sabrina lose everything she owned. But thank God for Chase, because he'd made a few calls and in about an hour, some guys from Three Men and a Truck had shown up. They'd loaded everything from the street and inside the house and taken it to a storage facility not far from Alexis's home. Alexis had quickly offered to pay for everything, but Chase had insisted he would take care of it.

Sabrina and Courtney were in the guest bedroom getting settled, and Alexis had just walked Chase to the front door. He leaned against it and pulled her toward him.

"You really didn't have to do all this," she said.

"No, but I wanted to."

"That's fine, but I really wish you'd let me pay you back."

Chase touched her lips with his forefinger. "I don't wanna hear another word about it. Your sister needed help, and I'm just glad I was there to do it."

"I'm glad, too, but I'm sorry you had to spend the rest of your day like this."

"It couldn't be helped. You were worried about your sister and your niece, and so was I."

"Words simply can't express how much this means to me. I was already crazy in love with you, but now I think I love you even more. You're such an unselfish man."

"I love you, too, and if you need anything at all, just call me. I mean that."

"I will," she said, kissing him.

Chase turned to open the door, but when he did, Sabrina stuck her head into the hallway.

"Um, Chase," she said. "I just wanted to thank you again for everything you did, and I'm sorry you had to waste all your time this evening."

"It wasn't a waste, and it was no trouble at all. You just take care of you and Courtney."

"I will," she said.

When Chase left, Alexis locked the door and walked down to the kitchen where Sabrina was. Sabrina gazed at the refrigerator and then cast her eye at Alexis as though she were ashamed. "Is it okay if I get a bottle of water?"

"Of course. You can have anything in there. I want you to make yourself at home."

Sabrina pulled out the water and sat at the island.

"Is Courtney still in the bedroom?"

"Yeah, she's lying across the bed watching television. She's really tired, though, so she might already be asleep."

Alexis sat down across from her. "You look tired, too."

"I am."

Alexis wanted to ask her why she was living the way she was, but she didn't want to sound judgmental. She also didn't want to argue with her sister.

"Are you hungry?" Alexis said.

"Not really."

The atmosphere was tense, so Alexis picked up the remote and switched on the small flat-screen on her kitchen counter. An old episode of *The Cosby Show* was on, and as Alexis watched it, she wished she and Sabrina were as close as the young sisters on the sitcom. Those sisters fussed and argued, too, but they always made up and life was good again between them.

Sabrina drank the last of her water. "I think I'm gonna go lie down, but thank you for letting us stay here."

"You're welcome. Before you head to bed, though, can I ask you something?"

"Not if it's about Melvin or why we got evicted, because I can't do that with you tonight, Alexis."

"No, it's about us. I wanna know why you've always had it in for me. Why we've never gotten along."

"I really don't wanna talk about that, either."

"Why?"

"Because I just don't. You and I have never been close, Alexis."

"But it's not right, and it's always bothered me."

"We're two totally different people, and you've always thought you were better than me."

"Why would you think that? Because I've always wanted something in life? Because I try my best to do the right thing?"

"No, because you're always throwing it in my face. You're always telling me what I need to do or what I shouldn't be doing."

"But only because I want you to have a better life."

"Maybe that's the reason you say those things now, but you were like this even when we were children. When I got bad grades in school, you told me I never studied enough. When I didn't make the cheerleading squad, you told me I hadn't practiced enough. When I didn't get a part in two of the school plays, you told me I hadn't memorized the lines well enough. Then, when I dropped out of high school, you told me I was just being lazy."

Alexis felt awful, because while she hadn't thought about those comments in years, she knew she'd made every single one of them. Not because she'd been trying to belittle her sister or because she thought she was better than her. It had actually been just the opposite. Alexis had made those comments because she'd truly believed Sabrina could do better and was capable of doing well with anything she wanted.

"I didn't realize my words had bothered you so much."

"Well, they did, and then once we became adults, you criticized me all the time. I kept telling you that not everyone is capable of doing all the things you've done, but you never listened. Then, as time went on, I resented you just a little more. Finally, I got to the place where I couldn't stand you at all."

"I'm really sorry. I really did think you were just being lazy and didn't want to work hard. Because unless a person has some sort of learning disability, it's hard for me to understand getting bad grades."

Sabrina gazed at her sister. "But that's just it, Alexis. I do have a learning disability. I'm dyslexic."

Alexis never took her eyes off Sabrina. "What do you mean?"

"I'm dyslexic. I always have been."

"How do you know?"

"About ten years ago I kept having problems on my job, so a coworker of mine told me I should get tested. She said I had a lot of the same symptoms as her son, and he'd just been diagnosed with dyslexia."

"Why didn't you tell me? Or at least you could've told Mom."

"By then, I just figured I'd deal with it on my own. I found a psychologist who helped me and taught me a lot, but I still struggle sometimes."

"You always knew so many things, though."

"That's because I listen well, and I watch a lot of news channels. That's how I learned so much. But when it came down to having to read, study, or take tests, I was completely lost."

"I can't believe none of your teachers noticed it."

"Well, if they did, they never said anything, and by the time I got to the eleventh grade, I just couldn't take it anymore. I was failing anyway, so I finally dropped out. From what I hear, most parents or teachers don't even consider that a child might be struggling with dyslexia. I mean, I daydreamed a lot, I zoned out in class while my teachers were talking, and my vision always seemed to be off. The letters and numbers never looked right to me, but when Mom and Dad took me to get an eye exam, they said my vision was fine."

"I am so, so sorry, Sabrina. I didn't know."

"I know you didn't. But all your comments over the years really hurt me, because you always made it sound like I was a failure at everything."

"All I can say is that I'm sorry, and that I won't ever do that to you again. I just didn't know."

"Well, now you do. I will admit one thing, though," Sabrina said. "I haven't always been the best mother to Courtney. Right after she was born, I really did leave her with Mom all the time just like you've said. But still, every time you complained about it, all that did was make me stay out more. It wasn't fair to Mom, though, and now I have to live with that. And I'll never be able to make it up to her," she spoke with watery eyes. "I'm such a mess. I got mixed up with the wrong man, and now we don't even have a place to live."

Alexis held Sabrina's hand. "You do have a place to live. You and Courtney will always have a place to live, and don't you ever forget that."

Sabrina sniffled, trying to hold back tears, but they fell anyway. "Thank you for taking us in. Thank you for always caring about Courtney. No matter how much you and I never got along, you have always been a good aunt to her. You've always loved her, and I appreciate that."

"I've always loved her, and I've always loved you, too. I never stopped."

"I never thought I'd be saying this," Sabrina said, slightly smiling, "but I'm so glad Courtney texted you. I wondered how you found out what was going on this afternoon, but then I saw it on my phone. I guess she was so upset, she forgot to delete it."

"I'm glad that Chase and I were just leaving the church."

"He's a really good guy."

"He is."

"Courtney told me that you're getting married in June."

"We were, but now we're doing it on Christmas Eve," Alexis said, suddenly thinking about Geneva again and what she might be up to.

"Wow, that's only two weeks away."

"I know, but with all the drama Chase's mother has caused, the sooner the better."

"She must be a real trip."

"You have no idea, but I'm getting ready to tell you all about it."

Chapter 22

Alexis and Sabrina had flipped through all Alexis's photo albums, and they'd laughed and cried for more than three hours. It was shortly after eleven a.m., and right after Sabrina had dropped Courtney off at school, she'd decided to call in sick. She'd told Alexis that she couldn't afford to miss a day without pay, but that she was also still too emotionally upset to be there. Alexis had explained that she would help her in any way she could, and that she didn't want her to worry.

"I haven't seen some of these pictures in years," Sabrina said, sipping some hot cocoa and turning more pages.

Alexis smiled at her but didn't say anything.

Sabrina must have felt her gaze. "What? Why are you looking at me like that?"

"You look so much like Mom."

"So do you."

"I know, but I don't think I ever noticed how much you look like her until now. I miss her so much, Sabrina."

"So do I. Mostly, though, I try not to think about it because it makes me sad. Sometimes Courtney will bring her up, and every now and then she'll still cry about her."

"These last five years have really been tough for me. I mean really, really tough."

"Nothing compares to losing a mother. Except maybe losing a child, because I could never imagine something happening to Courtney."

"Neither could I, and I'm just her aunt."

Sabrina gazed around the house. "I see you're not into Christmas decorating."

"Nope. I always enjoyed it at Mom's, but that was it. I haven't truly celebrated Christmas since she passed."

"Well, no matter how broke I was in December, every year I always made sure to put up our Christmas tree so that Courtney and I could decorate it. She and I always loved doing that together, but not this year I guess."

"I saw those guys bringing it out of your house."

Alexis wanted to offer to let them bring their tree to her home, but she wasn't sure she was ready for that. Then she thought about her mother's words again—how she had wanted Alexis to pick up where she left off and be happy.

"Why don't you put your tree up here?"

"No, that's okay. I know you don't like celebrating."

"I think it's time that I at least try. And maybe by having you and Courtney here with me, I won't feel as sad. So let's do it."

"Only if you want to."

"I do."

"Oh, and just so you know," Sabrina said, "I'm going to start looking for an apartment right away. I want to be out of here by the first."

"Of next month?"

"Yeah."

"You really don't have to rush. If you need to take a couple of months to save up some money, that'll be fine because I'll be moving in with Chase a day or two before we get married."

"We'll see. But my plan is to be gone by January."

"It's up to you, but I'm not planning to put my house on the market until February or so, anyway."

Sabrina turned a few more pages of the photo album she was looking at and then closed it. "I don't mean to change the subject, but I can't stop thinking about Chase's mother. She's such a terrible woman."

"Tell me about it," Alexis said.

"And you really think she's gonna try to sabotage your wedding?"

"I do. I'm not sure what she's planning, but come December twenty-fourth, she'll be ready and waiting. I just know it."

"Have you told Chase that?"

"No, and it wouldn't matter if I did, because he really believes his mother is done with trying to break us up. He knows she's still not happy about us getting married, but he doesn't think she'll do anything else."

"Maybe she won't. Maybe she'll just end up being an evil mother-in-law, and that'll be the end of it."

Alexis propped her elbow across the back of the sofa. "I doubt it, but I hope you're right. At least if she tries to stop us this time, I'll already be expecting it. There's no telling what she'll do, but if I had to guess, she'll either fake some serious illness right before the ceremony or she'll simply show up begging Chase not to marry me."

For the next hour, Alexis and Sabrina chatted more about Geneva and caught up on other things they'd never talked about before, until Alexis's phone rang. She smiled when she saw Chase's number.

"Hey, you," she said.

"Hi, baby. What's up?"

"Just sitting here with my sister, talking."

"Has she heard anything from that boyfriend of hers?"

"Not that I know of."

"Good. So, what are you guys doing for lunch?"

"Paula's coming by with some sandwiches. Actually, she should be here pretty soon."

"I wish I could see you, but with this new product launch, I just can't leave. Then, of course, with me being off yesterday, I missed a couple of important meetings and I need to be brought up to speed on them."

"No problem at all. You know I understand. Plus, I want you to get all your work done before the Christmas break so we can spend all our time together with *no* business interruptions."

"Yes, ma'am," he said, laughing. "The good news, too, is that the company will be closed December twenty-third through January first."

"So are we still taking a honeymoon?" she asked.

"Of course, but we might not be able to go until February or March because of my travel schedule toward the end of January. In the meantime, though, I was thinking maybe we could just spend our first two nights at the house on Christmas Eve and Christmas Day and then spend the next three days downtown Chicago. I can have someone here book the Peninsula for us."

"Sounds good to me," she said.

"Oh, and you haven't forgotten about our corporate Christmas party, have you? It's less than two weeks away."

"Of course not. I bought a dress for it over a month ago, and you know Paula definitely hasn't forgotten about it."

"I'm sure she hasn't," he said, laughing. "She practically begged to be invited, and I'm glad she and Rick will be there. It should be a really great time. We're giving out surprise bonuses, so everyone should be very happy."

"That's wonderful."

"Well, hey," he said, "I just wanted to hear your voice. I'll let you get back to your sister."

"I'll talk to you this evening. I love you, Chase."

"I love you, too, baby."

Alexis laid her phone down and heard the doorbell. Sabrina went to answer it, and Alexis was glad Sabrina was finally making herself at home.

Paula followed Sabrina into the room, speaking her mind. Needless to say, there was no sugarcoating involved. "I sure hope you're done with that low-down Melvin, girl. He's clearly not the one. Not to mention, you could do so much better than him."

Sabrina didn't even get mad. Actually, she shook her head and sort of laughed. Sabrina and Alexis hadn't spent a lot of time together in recent years, but Sabrina had still known Paula since they were children. Even though Alexis and Sabrina hadn't been close, Sabrina had always liked Paula.

"You haven't changed a bit, have you?" Sabrina said. "Still straight, no chaser."

"Girl, that's the only way to be," Paula said, setting the bag of food on the island and removing their sandwiches, chips, and sodas from it. "Especially when something really needs to be said. You've been going through this crap with Melvin for way too long, and I say it's time to move on."

Alexis shook her head at her friend. "Can you just pass me my tuna sandwich and stop all that?"

"What? Sabrina knows I'm tellin' the truth. She knows she needs to kick that fool to the curb."

"You're right," Sabrina finally said. "I'm through with him this time."

Alexis was shocked but thrilled. "Good for you."

Paula bit into her ham and turkey. "It's about time. And you know Lex and I are here for you. All you have to do is ask."

"Thank you for that," Sabrina said.

"You're welcome, and now all *we* have to do is get

your sister to the altar without any monster-in-law catastrophes."

Sabrina nodded. "I agree. Alexis told me what's been goin' on."

"That woman is crazy, Bri," Paula said. "And I don't trust her."

Alexis opened her soda. "Neither do I."

"When you're dealing with folks like Mrs. Dupont," Paula exclaimed, "you have to be ready at all times. People like her are plotting and scheming when everyone else is sleeping."

"Isn't that the truth," Alexis said.

Paula ate more of her sandwich. "You and Chase are gonna be fine, though. Only two weeks to go, and Mommy Dearest won't be able to stop anything."

"Well, if it hadn't been for you, Chase and I would still be broken up. So I really owe you, Paula."

"For what?"

"Bringing Pastor Black over here. I was so depressed, but talking with Pastor Black really made me think. He opened my eyes to so many things, and the next thing I knew, Chase was calling me and our engagement was back on."

"That's what friends are for, girl. Especially best friends."

"Best friends for life," Alexis said, and then looked at Sabrina. "And now I have my sister back, too. So it just doesn't get any better than that."

Chapter 23

 Borg-Freeman certainly knew how to throw a Christmas party, and Alexis was excited to be there. All the executives and department heads, along with their spouses and significant others, were dressed in perfectly cut tuxedos and elegant evening gowns, and the hors d'oeuvres were delectably satisfying. Over the years, Alexis had gone to many holiday parties in Mitchell, but The Tuxson's banquet facilities had to have been the most spectacular of all, and their catered food was the most divine. The Christmas decorations and exquisitely carved ice sculptures were simply stunning.

The mini orchestra played beautiful holiday carols, and everyone laughed and chatted with joy. Even Alexis was having a great time, and she was enjoying the celebration of Christmas again. She also thought about her sister and niece and smiled. They'd been very happy about including Alexis in their annual tree-trimming tradition, and she was grateful for the opportunity. They'd sung along with some of the best holiday tunes, drunk store-bought eggnog, and eaten Christmas cookies, and they'd joked around and laughed about the silliest things. It had only been the three of them, but by far, it had been the best family gathering in years. Alexis was also happy to know that Melvin hadn't done much calling, not as much as Alexis had expected him to, and that Sabrina was truly ready to move on without him the way she'd said. Alexis could tell that at times Sabrina felt sad and lonely, but for the most part, she was hanging in there and doing well.

"Hey, honey," Chase said, strutting toward her and looking as though he should be modeling for the cover of some national magazine. "I want you to meet someone." He wrapped his arm around her. "This is Jason Bartlett and his wife, Laura. Jason is our new CFO. Well, sort of new, anyway. Jason joined the company this past summer," he said. "And this is Alexis, my fiancée."

Alexis smiled and extended her hand, first to Laura and then to Jason. "It's a pleasure to meet you both."

"Likewise," Laura said, also smiling. "And what a gorgeous gown you have on. Red is certainly your color."

"You're very kind, and thank you for the compliment," Alexis said. "I love your dress, too."

"Why, thank you."

"It really is great to finally meet the woman the boss here speaks so highly of," Jason said.

Chase rubbed the side of Alexis's arm. "And it's all true, too. She's the best thing to ever happen to me."

"We're very happy for you both," Laura added.

There was something very calm and pleasant about Laura, and Alexis liked her already.

The four of them chatted for a few more minutes, and soon Paula and Rick walked in. Alexis had wondered when they would arrive, and to be honest, she was shocked that Paula hadn't gotten there before the doors opened. Paula loved attending these kinds of affairs, and she'd made it known to Chase a long time ago that she wanted to be included on as many Borg-Freeman guest lists as possible. Chase got a big kick out of Paula, and he had loved her since meeting her.

Chase gave formal introductions, and then the Bartletts left to go mingle with more staff members.

"This is so exciting, Chase," Paula said. "You guys really know how to put on a show."

"Yeah, it turned out pretty nice, didn't it?" he said.

"Please. Nice isn't even the word. This is incredible."

"And thanks a million for inviting us," Rick said, laughing. "Because if you hadn't, I think my girl here might've had a heart attack."

"Whatever, Rick," she said, and they all laughed.

Chase and Alexis made their rounds, offering more holiday well wishes, and Paula and Rick got something to eat. Then Chase and Alexis maneuvered their way to the front of the room, and Chase walked up the steps to the podium. When the music stopped, he began to speak.

"Good evening, everyone. Well, I first want to thank all of you for being here, and most important, I want to thank every employee here for all your hard work and dedication. I also want to thank all the spouses for tolerating some of the late hours many of us have been putting in over the last few months as we tirelessly prepared for the launch of our newest aerospace product. It just debuted this month, and I'm very happy to report that not only is it already a great success, but we'll be seeing lots of national coverage for it in the coming year. So again, I want to say thank you for a job well done."

Everyone applauded, and those holding champagne glasses lifted them toward Chase.

"My father, God rest his soul, would be very proud tonight and very happy to know that Borg-Freeman has experienced one of its most profitable years in history. So, that being said, every single employee, whether you're working at the executive level or in an entry-level position, will be receiving a very sizable check in the mail no later than Monday or Tuesday."

There was more applause, and it lasted much longer this time. There was also lots of conversation, and most people didn't seem to be quieting down. They were beyond excited.

"Maybe I should have saved that particular news for the very end of my speech," Chase said, laughing, and everyone else laughed along. "I'm just about finished, though, and actually, what I've done is save the best for last." He walked over to the top of the stairs and reached his hand out for Alexis. They walked back to the podium, and Chase held Alexis around her waist.

"As many of you know, I've finally found the woman of my dreams, and we're getting married."

"Hear, hear," some of the men said, and everyone applauded again.

"Thank you all so much. The one thing I haven't shared, though, is that instead of waiting until June, we're doing it three days from now, on Christmas Eve. And I tell you, I couldn't be happier. I've been blessed to run a great company, I have the best employees ever, and now my family life will finally be complete when I marry Alexis. So here's wishing all of you and your families a very merry Christmas and all of God's best in the new year."

Chase and Alexis clapped their hands along with everyone else and then stepped down from the platform. Folks walked over from every direction to congratulate them, and all was well until Alexis saw Geneva glide into the room dressed in a chic, full-length, bright green evening gown. She spotted Chase and Alexis immediately, but instead of acknowledging them, she strutted right past them, walked onto the stage, and stood in front of the microphone. Alexis knew the entire evening was about to be ruined, and that if Geneva was preparing to address the executives who worked for her own son, she was going to say a mouthful.

Paula and Rick made their way through the crowd.

"Oh my God, what is she up to?" Paula whispered to Alexis.

Alexis slightly hunched her shoulders, because she

hadn't a clue. Chase seemed hurt, angry, and embarrassed, and his mother hadn't even spoken yet. This was going to be a nightmare.

"May I have your attention, please," Geneva said, and the orchestra stopped playing again. "I'm really sorry to have to interrupt your party this evening, and if there had been any other way I wouldn't have. But as a mother, I'm obligated to do whatever I have to when it comes to the well-being of my son. I realize he's a grown man, and that he is a highly intelligent CEO whom you all have the utmost respect for, but for whatever reason, he's allowed this woman here," she said, pointing at Alexis, "to cloud his judgment."

Alexis stared at Geneva, and no one moved or made a sound. She was sure they were just as stunned as she was.

"So since I haven't been able to convince my son that he's marrying a very devious and duplicitous woman, I decided it was best to come ask each of you for your help. He simply won't listen to me, but once I tell you everything this woman has done, I'm sure you'll understand why I had to come speak publicly about it. I wanted to share this with you because of how much you care about Chase. I also couldn't just quietly sit back doing nothing while this woman brought down not just the Dupont family reputation, but also the reputation of this great company that my husband successfully ran for years. The company that all of you work for."

Now folks finally started to whisper, and Alexis's stomach tied in knots. Chase grabbed her hand and locked their fingers together, but she couldn't understand why he wasn't doing something to stop his mother. Why wasn't he rushing up to the podium and dragging her away from it? It was already apparent that she was planning to badmouth Alexis in the worst possible way, and once that happened, many of the employees would never see her the same. With these kinds of words coming from the former CEO's widow and the current CEO's mother, it wouldn't matter that Geneva was lying, because after this, questions would be left in everyone's minds and rumors would fly in all directions.

"You'll all be very shocked to hear this," Geneva said, pausing and attempting to squeeze out real tears. "But earlier this month, this same woman who claims to be so in love with my son burst into our home and attacked me. She threatened my life and told me that once she and Chase were married, she was going to make sure I never saw him again. She screamed at me, and she upset me to the point where I had to be rushed to the emergency room. I was in so much pain and my nerves were so shot, I thought I was going to die."

Whispers grew louder, and Alexis heard one woman say, "I knew she was only marrying him for his money. I knew it as soon as I heard about her."

"Please, please, please," Geneva said with both hands raised, "if you'll just give me two more minutes, I'll leave you to your party. The reason this woman has slithered her way into my son's life is because she grew up with nothing. She was raised up on the worst side of town, and now she's figured out a way to take our money. She's even talked my son into not making her sign a prenup agreement, even though we have millions of dollars."

Chase dropped Alexis's hand, went over to the short stairway, and walked back onstage. "Mother, I'm asking you to please leave."

"Honey, I'm doing this for your own good. I'm doing this because I love you, and because I have to protect you. This Alexis Fletcher woman is nothing more than a lying jezebel, and this all has to stop before she takes us to the cleaners."

"Lying jezebel?" Chase shouted. "Mother, you can't be serious. Not when you're the one who has all the skeletons."

"I have no idea what you're talking about," she said, preparing to go on with her monologue.

But Chase interrupted her. "Why are you doing this, Mother? Why are you trying to ruin my happiness?"

"Because you don't know any better. This woman came from the wrong side of the tracks, and you deserve better than that."

"Really? Then why did Daddy marry *you*? Why did my successful father marry a woman who grew up in a one-room shack down in Alligator, Mississippi? I was so shocked when I learned the truth about that, I had to look up the city to make sure it even existed."

"Oh my God," she said, reaching toward him. "Now this woman has made up a bunch of lies about me? And she's got you believing them?"

"These aren't lies, Mother, and Alexis knew nothing about this. I only found out myself a couple of years ago, and had you not pushed me, I would have taken every bit of it to my grave. I would have never confronted you about it. But you're a fraud, Mother."

"These are all lies, son. I swear," she said, pleading with him. "You have to believe me."

Alexis didn't know what to say or think, but she desperately wanted to grab Chase's arm and pull him off the stage. She wanted to drag him out of the room altogether. He was so enraged that he'd forgotten about all his colleagues being in the room, and that this was the company's annual Christmas party—he'd forgotten that he was the CEO, and that everyone in the city was going to hear about this.

But Chase was on a roll, and Alexis knew no one could stop him. Not even her.

"And then, Mother, imagine my surprise when you kept saying Alexis hadn't gone to the right colleges, and that she wasn't good enough for me. I couldn't believe it, because you never even graduated from high school yourself, let alone attended college. All these years, you'd told me that your parents were dead, that you were born in Atlanta, and that you'd graduated from Spelman College. You even have a fake diploma from Spelman in your home office, and I can remember times when you flew to Atlanta for what you said were alumni events."

Beads of perspiration lined Chase's forehead, and Alexis could tell he was getting angrier by the millisecond.

Chase tightened his face and stared at his mother. "But you know what was worst of all, Mother? Finding out that your real name isn't even Geneva. It's Essie Mae. And just in case you're interested, your mother is alive and well, and I've been sending her money every month since I met her. I've also been taking care of your two younger sisters. And all this time, Mother, you told me you were an only child. You lied about everything."

Alexis pulled Chase by his arm, and although he resisted at first, he finally gave in and walked away with her. They left the room and then the building, but Chase said nothing. He was numb, and Alexis knew things between him and his mother would never be the same. *He* would never be the same, and it would take a lot of healing for him to get past this.

It would take a miracle for him to ever trust his mother again.

Chapter 24

$\mathcal{I}$t was Christmas Eve, only three days since the party fiasco, but Alexis and Chase were still getting married. Alexis had thought maybe it would be best for them to wait a few more weeks so that Chase could deal with all the unresolved feelings he had toward his mother, but he wouldn't hear of it. She'd even tried to get him to go see his mom, but whenever she brought that up, he acted as though he hadn't heard her. He wouldn't outright ignore her, but he'd change the subject, caress the side of her face, or do anything he could think of as long as he didn't have to respond to her comment. There was no denying that Geneva had treated Alexis horribly from day one, but because of all the Christian values Alexis's mother had taught her, Alexis couldn't imagine Chase cutting off his mother for good. She understood how angry and hurt he was—everyone who knew about his mother's lies and deceit understood—but Geneva Dupont, aka Essie Mae Jackson, was still the woman who had brought him into this world. Alexis was sure Geneva still loved and cherished him, even though Chase no longer believed that.

But now here they stood in the presence of God, family members, and friends, preparing to take lifelong vows. Chase wore a stylish black suit with a black-and-white-striped tie, a white handkerchief, and a white rose boutonnière, and Alexis wore a pure white satin jacket and skirt with a double-strand pearl necklace. She also wore pearl earrings and a matching bracelet, and her hair was pulled back in a chignon. Her Christmas-themed wedding bouquet was made mostly of white roses, with a few red ones sprinkled throughout and a hint of greenery.

One of Alexis's favorite soloists at the church sang "Silent Night" in honor of Alexis's mother, and Alexis wasn't sure the song had ever sounded more serene and moving.

Pastor Black smiled at Chase and Alexis. "I must say, this is a very blessed day and a very happy one. It gives me great joy to be able to perform this ceremony for two truly wonderful individuals who love God as well as each other. So let us begin.

"Dearly beloved, we are gathered here today in the presence of these witnesses to join Chase William Dupont the Third and Alexis Marie Fletcher in holy matrimony, which is commended to be honorable among all men, and therefore is not to be entered into by anyone unadvisedly or lightly, but reverently, discreetly, advisedly, and solemnly. Into this holy estate, these two persons present now come to be joined. If any person can show just cause why they may not be joined together, let them speak now or forever hold their peace."

Alexis quickly thought about Chase's mother again and how she'd expected that this would be the day Geneva would come forward to try to stop their marriage. But as it had turned out, she'd had much bigger plans and had carried them out at the party.

"Who presents this woman to be married to this man?"

Sabrina stepped forward. "On behalf of those who are with us, and my parents who have gone before us, I give my love, support, and blessing to this union."

Alexis smiled at Sabrina; they both blinked back tears and held each other.

Alexis quietly said, "Thank you."

Now, Courtney walked toward them. "I'm so happy for you, Aunt Lexi." She hugged her aunt tightly and also her new uncle.

Pastor Black continued. "No other human ties are more tender, no other vows are more sacred than these you are about to assume. You are entering into the holy estate which is the deepest mystery of experience, and which is the very sacrament of divine love. Chase, will you have Alexis to be your lawfully wedded wife, to live together after God's ordinance in the holy estate of matrimony? Will you love her, comfort her, honor and keep her, in sickness and in health, and forsaking all others, keep yourself only for her so long as you both shall live?"

Chase gazed into Alexis's eyes. "I will."

"Alexis, will you have Chase to be your lawfully wedded husband, to live together after God's ordinance in the holy estate of matrimony? Will you love him, comfort him, honor and keep him, in sickness and in health, and forsaking all others, keep yourself only for him so long as you both shall live?"

"I will," she said, gazing back at him.

Pastor Black asked everyone to bow their heads and close their eyes, and he spoke a wedding prayer over Chase and Alexis. Then he asked them to hold hands and recite their vows.

Chase gazed at Alexis again. "Not once did I ever believe it was possible to find my true soul mate...until I met you. From the moment I first saw you, I knew you were special and that you were going to be my wife. The woman I would love and spend the rest of my life with. The woman I would always be able to trust and depend on. You make me smile, you make me laugh, and you give me the best kind of peace. I love you with all my heart...I love you with everything in me, and I am yours forever."

Alexis wiped tears from Chase's cheeks and then wiped her own. She was so in love with him that she could barely keep a straight face. She wanted to cry out loud with happiness, but she calmly began her vows.

"From the moment Pastor Black introduced us, I knew you were the man God had created for me. To be honest, I fell in love with you so quickly, it sort of frightened me. But it wasn't long before I realized how genuine our love truly was. You are every breath I take, and I never want to spend even one day without you. You are my heart and soul...my everything. I love you, I thank God for you, and I am yours forever."

Pastor Black asked for their rings and performed the ring vows portion of the ceremony. Then Chase and Alexis slipped the wedding bands on each other's fingers.

"For as much as Chase and Alexis have consented together in holy matrimony and have witnessed the same before God and this company, by the authority committed unto me as a minister of the Gospel of Jesus Christ, I declare that Chase and Alexis are now husband and wife, according to the ordinance of God and the law of the state of Illinois—in the name of the Father, and of the Son, and of the Holy Spirit. Amen."

Alexis looked over at Paula, who was crying silently, smiling and holding Rick's hand. As Paula had suspected, Rick had surprised her with an engagement ring this morning, and Alexis couldn't be happier for her.

The soloist sang "The Lord's Prayer," and Chase and Alexis never took their eyes off each other. Alexis thought about her mother, who she wished could physically be there, but knowing that her mother's spirit was present in her heart gave her peace. On the other hand, she was sure Chase was thinking about his mother, too, and Alexis prayed they'd be able to salvage their relationship.

When the soloist took her seat on one of the pews, Pastor Black prayed again and then said, "On this most precious Christmas Eve day, I present to you Mr. and

Mrs. Chase Dupont the Third. Chase, you may kiss your bride."

They embraced and kissed for the first time as husband and wife, and life was good. Alexis knew Christmas wasn't until tomorrow, but this had already turned out to be her best Christmas ever. It was a blessing all around.

Epilogue

Three Months Later

*M*oving to a totally different house had taken a bit of time to get used to, but Alexis finally felt right at home. Of course, she'd never felt the least bit uncomfortable or like she was a stranger in Chase's house, but a change in residence had required a certain amount of adjustment. The good news, though, was that as long as she was with Chase, she was happy anywhere. In fact, they'd just gotten back from Jamaica, and they'd had the best time there, too. They'd eaten well, relaxed on the beach, and made love every single day the way they'd planned, and while Chase had originally preferred going to Italy, he hadn't wanted to leave the islands. He'd been so impressed and so pleased with the entire atmosphere, he was already suggesting they go again in six months. Alexis certainly didn't have a problem with that, and she looked forward to it.

It was still great to be back in the States, however, and

great to be doing more prep work for her speaking engagement with C&G Pharmaceuticals. Time had flown by very quickly, and before she knew it, she'd be on a plane next month to their conference.

Alexis looked up from her desk when she thought she heard the doorbell ringing. Since it was Saturday, Margaret was off for the weekend, and Chase was out picking up lunch for them, but Alexis wasn't expecting any company. When the bell rang again, though, she left her office, walked down the long, carpeted hallway and the winding staircase, and looked through the upper part of the frosted-glass double doors. She knew she wasn't just seeing things, but she peered at Geneva again just to be sure it was her. Alexis was nervous and shocked all at the same time, but she opened the door.

"Hi, Alexis," Geneva said, half smiling. She was dressed as immaculately as ever, but she looked tired, and like she hadn't been sleeping. "I know it's very impolite of me to show up unannounced, but I wondered if I could come in and talk to you. I promise I won't take much of your time."

"Sure," Alexis said, opening the door all the way.

They walked through the entryway and, ironically, sat in the same two chairs they'd sat in the day Alexis had come there trying to make peace.

Geneva set her handbag on the table between them and sighed. "I'm not even sure where to begin, but I think the first thing I have to do is apologize. Alexis, I am so very sorry for everything. I'm sorry for the way I treated you, for all the lies I told about you, and for trying to force my son to break up with you."

Alexis nodded.

"You must think I'm the most awful person in the world, and I certainly don't blame you for that. But having my own son expose my pathetic past and disclose all my lies to everyone, well... that was a rude awakening. Even worse, the pain and disgust I saw on his face that night hurt me to the core, and I know my relationship with him has changed forever. And it's all because of how ashamed I've always been about where I came from. My mother had me when she was only fifteen, and from the time I was born, she stood on corners, selling her body. But then, when I turned sixteen, she made me start sleeping with men, too. She forced me to do it for nearly a whole year," Geneva said, and Alexis cringed.

Her mother-in-law had been through much more than Alexis would have ever imagined, and it explained a lot.

Geneva stroked her hair to the side. "It was awful, and I knew I had to leave there. I also knew I could never go back. And I didn't. I moved to Atlanta, changed my name, and worked two waitressing jobs. I struggled for five long, hard years, but one day my luck finally changed. An extremely handsome, wealthy-looking man came into one of the high-end restaurants I worked at, and it was love at first sight for both of us. I was twenty-two, and he was thirty-seven. Like Chase, he'd recently become one of the youngest Fortune 500 CEOs in the country, and I lied and told him that I'd just graduated from Spelman. I told him I hadn't been able to find a full-time job in the business world yet, and that's why I was working where I was."

Alexis listened, surprised at how forthcoming Geneva was about everything.

"Anyway, Chase the Second never suspected that I was born in some tiny town in Mississippi...or that I was lying about every aspect of my life. That is, until one day he decided to dig through my background and discovered the truth about everything. It was right after Chase had turned ten, and from that point on, our marriage became loveless and we slept in separate bedrooms. Publicly, we portrayed ourselves as a loving couple, but at home we rarely even spoke unless it was about Chase," she said with sad eyes. "The reason I'm sharing all of this with you, Alexis, is because the bottom line is that for years, no one has really loved me except my son. So when I saw how genuinely in love he was with you and how genuinely you loved him back, I worried that I would be shut out of Chase's life completely. I also resented you because of your degrees and because you'd made a life for yourself...without having to marry for money the way I did. I did love my husband, but every time I saw you, it reminded me of who I wished I'd been able to become on my own. You reminded me of all the things I hadn't done in life, and I envied you for it."

"I'm really sorry," Alexis said. "I had no idea."

"Still, I had no right causing so much trouble for you and Chase or for creating such a scandal for him to deal with at Borg-Freeman. But what I'm hoping is that maybe you and I can start over. I'm hoping you can find it in your heart to forgive me. Let me try to become the kind of mother-in-law you deserve."

"I forgave you the night of the Christmas party, Geneva. I did it because it was right, and because of something my mom once told me. She said that when people thrive on hurting others, they do it because they're hurting inside themselves."

"Thank you for forgiving me, and although I never met your mother, I'm sure she was right."

When the security system chimed, they both looked toward the doorway. Alexis wasn't sure how Chase was going to react when he saw his mother, but she prayed he wouldn't say anything out of the way. However, Chase never so much as came in the room.

Geneva seemed nervous but didn't comment, so Alexis finally got up and went into the kitchen.

"What is she doing here?" he asked, opening what looked like a container of chicken Alfredo.

"She came to apologize."

"Really? Well, good for her."

"Baby, you really need to hear her out."

"Why? Don't you think we heard enough at the Christmas party? It was one thing for her to lie about who she was, but to try to break us up simply because she decided you weren't good enough? I don't think so. And anyway, what mother would stoop low enough to hurt her own child that way? She knew how much I loved you, and how happy you made me, but all she cared about was herself. And worse than that, baby, what decent human being walks away from her own mother and doesn't have anything to do with her for decades? She never called her or went to see her once."

Alexis touched his arm. "Honey, she had her reasons. I hate having to tell you this, but your grandmother was a prostitute...and she turned your mom into one as well. She made her sleep with all kinds of men until your mom finally couldn't take it anymore."

Chase set down the knife and fork he was holding but never looked up at Alexis. He paused for a few seconds and then said, "Do you believe her?"

"I do. I saw it in her eyes when she was telling me."

"How old was she?" he asked.

"What do you mean?"

"When my grandmother first made her sleep with those men?"

"Sixteen."

Chase closed his eyes, and Alexis went over and held him.

"Baby, I know this isn't easy, but do you know what I would give to have my mother here with me again? Just to see her face. Just to physically touch her. You only get one mother, and life can be very short. A whole lot shorter than you're counting on. I mean, what if something happened to your mom, and you'd never allowed her the chance to make things up to you? You would never forgive yourself for that."

Chase rested his forehead against hers. "I love you so much, baby."

"I love you, too."

"And although I know I've told you this before, I'm so sorry I didn't tell you about my mother's secrets. I'm sorry you had to find out the way you did, because I never wanna keep anything from you. But I just couldn't tell you about all her lies. I was so ashamed."

"I understand, and that's all behind us now. We have to move forward."

"I know, but even when she told all those lies on you, deep down I knew what she was capable of. But again, I still didn't wanna believe she would tell lies that would hurt me directly."

"You don't have to keep apologizing for that. What's important is that we never stopped loving each other and that everything worked out."

"You have such a forgiving heart. And thank you for hanging in there."

Alexis held both sides of his face. "You're welcome. Now, go talk to your mother."

Chase kissed her and left the kitchen.

Alexis watched him leave and smiled when she thought about the Christmas prayer she'd written. God had given her everything she'd asked for, and she was grateful. But now she prayed for something else: a close relationship with her mother-in-law. She knew Geneva had done everything she could to hurt her, but Alexis still believed that God had brought them together for

a reason. He never, ever made mistakes, and He was always true to His Word—and Alexis depended on that.
She trusted Him with her life, and it was for that reason
she knew she would be fine. They would all be fine as a
family, and that was all that truly mattered.

Acknowledgments

As always, I thank God for absolutely everything. Your grace and mercy have made ALL the difference in my life, and it is the reason I love, honor, trust, and depend on You, no matter what. To my wonderful husband, Will, for all the love and support you have given me for twenty-four years—I love you from the depths of my heart and soul; to my brothers, Willie, Jr., and Michael Stapleton for all the wonderful childhood Christmas memories as well as the many laughs we share today—I love you both so very much; to my stepson and daughter-in-law, Trenod and Tasha Vines-Roby, and your children; to the rest of my family (Tennins, Ballards, Lawsons, Stapletons, Youngs, Beasleys, Haleys, Romes, Greens, Robys, Garys, Shannons, Normans, and everyone else I'm related to); to my amazing first cousin and fellow author, Patricia Haley-Glass; my two best friends, Kelli Tunson Bullard and Lori Whitaker Thurman; my dear cousin, Janell Green; and my spiritual mother, Dr. Betty Price—I love each and every one of you so very much.

To my publishing attorney, Ken Norwick; to my amazing publisher, Hachette/Grand Central Publishing: Jamie Raab, Beth de Guzman, Linda Duggins, Elizabeth Connor, Scott Rosenfeld, the entire sales and marketing teams, and everyone else at GCP; to my extremely talented freelance team: Connie Dettman, Shandra Hill Smith, Luke LeFevre, Pam Walker-Williams, and Ella Curry—thank you all for everything! To all the bookstores and retailers who carry my work, and every newspaper, radio station, TV station, and website or blog that promotes it, and to all the fabulous book clubs that continually choose my books as your monthly selections— thank you a thousand times over.

To the wonderful people who make my writing career possible—**my kind, loyal, and truly supportive readers**. I love you dearly, and I am forever grateful.

Much love and God bless you always,

Kimberla Lawson Roby

E-mail: kim@kimroby.com
Facebook: www.facebook.com/kimberlalawsonroby
Twitter: www.twitter.com/KimberlaLRoby

Reading Group Guide

1. Do you believe prayer has to be formal or follow a certain structure? Or can it be as simple as talking to God from your heart while driving down the road?

2. If you have ever lost a loved one, what helped you deal with the grief? What advice can you give others trying to cope with their own loss? What can you advise in terms of coping with family holidays after the loss of a loved one?

3. Are all losses created equal? Is losing a spouse different from losing a parent? What about losing a child or a sibling? Why or why not?

4. Do you think Alexis was clinically depressed or just feeling sad? Is there a difference and, if so, what is it?

Do you think there is anything else Alexis could have tried doing to help herself? Was Paula right to intervene? What do you do personally when you're feeling down to cheer yourself back up?

5. Was Alexis right to get involved with Courtney and her parents? Should she have handled the situation differently, or done anything else for her niece? If you believe so, please explain.

6. What do you think about the way Chase dealt with his mother? Could he—or should he—have done anything differently? Was it fair of Alexis to ask him to talk to his mother?

7. Have you ever had a Geneva in your life—a mother-in-law or mother of a significant other, or even a jealous friend who tried to come between you and someone you loved? If so, how did you deal with that person?

8. Both Geneva and Alexis disapproved of the person someone in their family was dating. Have you ever disapproved of the person someone in your family was seeing? Is it ever okay to speak up and get involved when you feel this way? If so, when? What are some appropriate ways to handle the situation?

9. Do you believe Alexis and Geneva will ever have a close relationship?

10. How do you define the spirit of Christmas? If you were to write your own Christmas prayer, what would it say?